silent STORMS

silent STORMS

Ariella Schiller

Copyright © 2016 by Israel Bookshop Publications

ISBN 978-1-60091-480-5

Book design by Elisheva Appel

Distributed by:
Israel Bookshop Publications
501 Prospect Street / Lakewood, NJ 08701
Tel: (732) 901-3009 / Fax: (732) 901-4012
www.israelbookshoppublications.com / info@israelbookshoppublications.com

Printed in United States of America

Distributed in Israel by:
Shanky's
Petach Tikva 16
Jerusalem
972-2-538-6936

Distributed in Europe by:
Lehmanns
Unit E Viking Industrial Park
Rolling Mill Road,
Jarrow, Tyne & Wear NE32 3DP
44-191-430-0333

Distributed in Australia by:
Gold's Book and Gift Company
3- 13 William Street
Balaclava 3183
613-9527-8775

Distributed in South Africa by:
Kollel Bookshop
Northfield Centre
17 Northfield Avenue
Glenhazel 2192
27-11-440-6679

To Meir:
The reason people say the husbands I write up are not believable.
Thank you — I'm sure the two words
have never been more insufficient in all of time.
Here's to writing a story all of our own...

ACKNOWLEDGMENTS

A second book is very different than a first. A first book is almost like birthing a child. For months you work and prepare, but you don't really believe anything will come out of it. And then, poof, there it is, cradled in your hands. All soft pages, hard covers, and that intoxicating scent of ink. Suddenly, anything is possible.

Which leads to a second book. And a second book is an affirmation. It's an announcement to the world that you haven't been deterred, that writing a book has been such a wonderful experience that you've come back for, well, seconds. A second book says that the response has been wonderful, the opportunities exhilarating, and the fans unbelievably enthusiastic and encouraging. So, in a way, a second book is a thank you. Thank you to all those who have supported me in my writing. Thank you to the writers and bloggers who have written up reviews, to the readers who have sent in their love, to the friends who have taken time out of their life to curl up and read my brainchild.

A second book is a triumph. It's an answer to those annoying voices in my head that tell me, constantly and consistently, that my one book was a fluke, that I'll never be as good as other authors, that I should try to focus when people are speaking to me, instead of writing up what they are saying in my mind.

So you can see why I'm excited...

But before I invite you to dive into my affirmation, thank you, and triumph, there are some people who must be mentioned. *The Jewish Press*, of course, and Chumi Friedman, for serializing this book in its earlier stages. Thank you so much for the chance to share my words with the world. To Israel Bookshop, Malkie Gendelman, and the crew: The amount of dedication and devotion you've shown to this book, to my work, to my voice, is unbelievable. Thank you so much for everything; I think it came out amazing.

To my Abba and Ema: Words once again fail me. At least I know who my biggest fans are! Thank you for every word of encouragement, every introduction as "my daughter, the writer," every brainstorm and compliment.

To my sisters: Rivka and Tzipora, thanks for the advice, guidance, and tutorials on anorexia, being a social worker, and mental health counseling. The rest of you: you all deserve to be licensed, as well! Thank you for listening to me, encouraging me, and for the laughs and love.

And of course, Ahron Yosef, for introducing *Dreams Delayed* to your friends. Think *Silent Storms* will be a hit with them, too?

And to Tatty, Mommy, and the gang: Every day spent as a Schiller is an adventure and a privilege. I love you all so much!

Sabba, thank you for always being there, as a listening ear or just a guiding hand. I love you so much…

To my coworkers and the whole office crew: Thank you! For teaching me that the written word actually has rules! And for being the sort of friends that only come from arguing over ellipsis…

And to my friends: Each one of you is so special to me. I love you guys…

And to my Yaakov! My beautiful, sweet big boy. I am so proud of the person you are growing up to be. Maybe one day you'll actually read my books, but in the meantime, thanks for keeping me company while I write. I love you!

And last but not least, to the *Ribono Shel Olam*, Who has blessed me with more good than I could ever imagine, even within my most creative brainstorming sessions. Thank You for everything I have. May I use it all to make You proud.

Now you can dive in. Enjoy!

PROLOGUE

The music was reminiscent of the ocean in the way it rose and fell, like waves hungrily swallowing everything before them, then crashing, subdued, back into the water. He played like a man possessed, barely pausing to breathe, not stopping to eat, just playing, playing, trying to play the pain away...

Hours passed before she came in. "I... Did you say something?" she asked him, her brow wrinkled.

He looked at her, his reed still in his mouth.

"Oh," she said. She tried again. "It's just...I thought...I thought I heard a cry, coming from here." She looked pained, and in her pain, there was a touch of confusion, although it was mostly grief, with just a tinge of fear.

He felt the anger rising, rising, until he would surely burst. *Channel it*, he reminded himself. "I...I need to play," he said abruptly.

Her eyes shuttered. "Okay," she whispered.

He watched her leave, her shoulders hunched. Even her posture had been taken from her. And then, when he saw how much it was her pain, too, and not just his, he could take it no more. With a strength he didn't know he had, he lifted the wooden flute. Summoning all the pain and rage churning inside him, he bore down and — *snap!*

He stared down in wonderment at the splintered halves of his beloved instrument. Only then did he cry, his sobs billowing to take the place of the music. And, like an ocean's waves, they, too, engulfed him.

CHAPTER ONE

The door was painted a soft pink. This seemed ironic, somehow, as the scene behind would surely be a demonstration of bright and angry reds. She faced it, contemplating this, one hand poised on the door handle. She steeled herself, took a deep breath, and knocked lightly.

"Aviva?" she called softly. "Can I come in?"

Silence and then, "Yeah."

She rolled her eyes at this less-than-enthusiastic response and pushed open the door. The shades were pulled down, the room was dark, and it had the lingering antiseptic odor of a hospital room. She turned toward the bed, where the faint glow of an iPod was emanating from under the covers.

"Aviva."

She waited a moment, and when no answer was forthcoming, she walked over to the shades on the barred windows and flung them open. Then she marched over to the light switch and flicked it on. Only then did she turn toward the bed, where a very angry teenage girl was blinking at her.

"What. Do. You. Think. You. Are. Doing?" Aviva asked through gritted teeth.

She flicked back her *sheitel* and sat down primly at the edge of the bed. "I don't like being ignored," she said airily. The girl stared at her, and she took pity. "Oh, Aviva." She sighed. "Why?"

Aviva kept staring at her, which gave her a chance to study the girl. Her blue eyes were dull and seemed to be taking up the entirety of her small, white face. They were further enunciated by purple-black crescents smudged underneath, indicating sleepless nights. Her lips were cracked and dry, and her cheekbones were so sharp, they seemed to protrude right out of her face.

She swallowed down the bile that was suddenly rising in the back of her throat. Time to turn off her emotions.

"Aviva," she said briskly. "Your counselor said you are, and I quote, 'not cooperating.' Let's see..." She flicked through her notes. "Stormed out of group therapy. Fudged the daily weigh-in. Silent treatment during counseling. And refusal to eat in the dining room..." Here she paused and waited. And waited. After five minutes, just when she was about to give up and walk out, the silence was broken.

"What do *you* know?!" The words were spit out with such venom that she recoiled.

"I'm sorry?" she said politely.

Aviva flung her head upward and stared at her. "I said, what do *you* know?! I'll bet you're one of those people who've had a perfect figure since the day you were born! You were probably never fat a day in your life!" Aviva stared at her accusingly and folded her arms, blue veins spider-webbing across her translucent skin, not realizing that they mimicked the cracks that were now spreading across her social worker's shattered heart.

"You're right, Aviva," she said quietly. "I've never been fat a day in my life. Have a good night." And she gently patted the girl's tense shoulder before walking toward the door, taking extra care to flick off the light before leaving.

ﻉ

SHE LEANED AGAINST THE ELEVATOR WALL and took deep, calming breaths, determined to keep the tears at bay. The doors pinged, and she quickly jammed on her sunglasses before anyone recognized the telltale sheen in her eyes.

Mrs. Rappaport entered the elevator, her arms overflowing with papers, her phone ringing, and her briefcase dangling precariously over one elbow.

"Oh, hello, Gali," she said brightly, smiling at the social worker.

Gali pasted a smile onto her face as she greeted the facility's supervisor. "How are you, Mrs. Rappaport? You look overloaded; can I help you with those papers?"

The supervisor smiled. "No, no, I'm good. Thank you. Just rushing to pick up my daughter from her swimming lesson, and my son from *cheder* for a doctor's appointment. Then I have to make dinner, while still getting these progress reports out tonight! And, of course, the baby's teething, so there's not too much hope for a good night's sleep, even after I get everything done... But I guess that's life, right?" She smiled disarmingly.

Gali smiled back and exited the elevator at the next floor, before Mrs. Rappaport would remember whom she was talking to and start stuttering a mortified apology.

Oh, great, this floor was the parking garage. Okay, then, she'd take the long way out. She left the garage and walked around the perimeter of the building before finding herself, finally, at the bus stop on the corner. Thankfully, Mrs. Rappaport was nowhere to be seen, and the sun was shining brightly.

She took a calming breath and fished through her bag for her bus card. She looked up just in time to catch a young woman staring at her. Gali ignored her, but then she noticed the woman running her hands down her wrinkled black skirt while hastily combing her *sheitel* bangs with her fingers. Gali sighed inwardly, hating the anger she knew was rising inside her stomach. But what was she supposed to do?

The woman was now determinedly not looking at Gali, her body turned at least 180 degrees away from her. Gali didn't need to be a social worker to know that the woman was obviously intimidated by her, not to mention jealous, as well.

Why?! Gali wanted to yell. *Why are you jealous? Because of my perfect* sheitel? *My flawless makeup? This pretty, expensive outfit? You want it? Take it! Take it all; I'll gladly trade with you any day. Take my designer purse for the diaper bag dangling off of your shoulder. Take my cashmere sweater for your black t-shirt with spit-up stains on it. Take my suede skirt for your wrinkled, smudged one that obviously had a child sitting on it at some point during the day. Take my perfect* sheitel *that's never been yanked sideways by little hands, and my makeup that has never been kissed off by little faces. Take it all, please! Oh, suddenly you're not so anxious to switch places with me? Didn't think so...*

And finally the tears came, as her torrent of unspoken words consumed her. But she was an expert at hiding them by now. She ducked her head into her bag, dabbed her face, pinched her cheeks, blew her nose, and was perfectly composed by the time the bus came roaring down the street two minutes later.

Chapter Two

Gali slid a pan of brownies into the oven, humming along with the CD playing in the surround sound system. Baking soothed her. There was something so rewarding in creating something tangible. Besides, Dovi loved her brownies.

She smiled at the memory of the first time she'd baked brownies for her husband. She'd accidentally left out the sugar, and the bewildered and disappointed look on his face when he tried eating a warm, chocolaty piece was priceless. Now it was twelve years later, and she'd become a pro at making his favorite dessert. He, in turn, had become a pro at masking his disappointment, though today's dealt cards were much harsher than a sugarless dessert...

Gali sighed and went to the sink to wash her hands.

DOVI BREEZED INTO THE HOUSE with a cheery hello and flung his hat onto the leather sofa.

She came out of the kitchen, smiling. "Supper's almost rea—"

"You've been crying," he interrupted her.

She stared at him. "How do you always *know*?"

He smiled mysteriously, but then grew serious. Leading her toward the couch, he asked, "Why, Gals? What happened today?"

"I'll tell you," she said, "but not there. Come to the kitchen. I have fresh brownies and iced coffee..." She let the offer dangle.

"Sold," he said, following her out of the living room.

They settled down at the breakfast bar, and Gali told him the whole story, starting with her anorexic client and moving on to the young mother at the bus stop.

"It's like everyone thinks they have me all figured out," she said in frustration. "They have me in this box — thin, pretty, nice clothes, happy smile on her face — and they think, okay, she must have the perfect life. As if that's true. As if I have *no idea* what pain is all about."

Then she laid her head down on the countertop and cried as if her heart would break. Her husband looked on helplessly, while the iced coffee melted into a lukewarm, brown liquid.

જ

SHE WAS PUTTING AWAY the last of the dishes when the phone rang. She checked the caller ID, and when she saw the name *Rappaport*, her heart sank.

"Don't get the phone," she called out to Dovi, who was learning in the next room. "Let it go to the machine, please!"

The CD was playing again, and Dovi was chanting a *Tosafos* out loud, but the volume on the answering machine was high enough for both of them to hear the message being recorded.

"Hi, Gali. It's Shaindy Rappaport. How are you?" The voice was hesitant and tense, not at all like the vivacious, confident woman Gali knew from work. "I just wanted to say that I am so, so sorry for what I said in the elevator earlier... I was speaking without thinking, and if I caused you any *tza'ar* at all, I hope you can be *mochel* me... I'm, uh, not used to filtering what I say, and I'm afraid today I learned my lesson at last. So have a good night...and I'm sorry, again. Really." *Click.*

Gali, who had frozen at the sound of the supervisor's voice, regained her sense of motion and walked slowly into the living room, where Dovi sat, staring up at the ceiling. The two looked at each other, and then, inexplicably, burst out laughing.

Gali sank down onto the couch, and the two of them laughed for a long, long time, while dusk gave way to nighttime outside and the moon and stars emerged, lending light to an otherwise dark, dark world.

GALI SIFTED THROUGH HER EMAILS, humming quietly. As she'd done countless times over the years of her marriage, she murmured a fervent thank you to Hashem for her husband. Laughing today's difficult experience off with Dovi had made her feel much better; more than that, she was actually feeling *good*. She loved her work, she loved her home, she had Dovi... So, she didn't have children yet. So, one of her clients was driving her up the wall...things could be worse. She smiled, mocking her own endless positivity, but proud of it as well.

Her humming got louder as she opened an email from her younger sister. Five little faces smiled up at her, freckles, pigtails, and bows all in abundance. She froze and stared at the photo for a while, her heart thudding. Then, quietly, she logged out of her computer, pushed her chair back, and went off to bed, her humming and positive thoughts now nothing but a ghostly memory.

CHAPTER THREE

G ali sauntered down the aisle in the supermarket, pushing her wagon in front of her. She loved Thursdays. More specifically, she loved Shabbos, and since Thursday was the prelude to that, well, then she loved Thursdays.

She put a package of fresh snap peas into her cart and paused to examine the exotic mushrooms they had on display. Dovi loved mushrooms; Gali did not. She found them rubbery when cooked, and tasteless when not. Besides, as she liked to point out to Dovi, a mushroom was a *fungus*. Why would someone want to eat a fungus? Still, she had a great recipe for stuffed mushrooms, and these did look unusual... She picked up one of them to examine and heard a *tsk-tsk* from behind her.

"Honestly, can you believe these prices? I mean, they've raised the cost on everything! How on earth are you supposed to be able to afford all this, hmm? I mean, first the price of formula goes skyrocketing, then diapers, and now vegetables! I mean, really!"

Gali turned around and looked at the woman who had decided to use her as a sounding board for her frustration. The woman looked to be in her thirties and appeared very put together. Though Gali had learned — the hard way — never to judge someone based on external appearances, this well-dressed woman did not seem to be too strained from the "skyrocketing prices" of groceries. She was tapping one manicured finger against her designer purse while an overdressed little girl sat in the front of her wagon, pulling at the rather enormous flower that was pinned in her short, blond curls.

Gali smiled at the little girl. "What a cutie," she said to the mother, who was now looking Gali up and down.

Apparently approving of what she saw, the woman continued her little speech. "What? Oh, thank you...Tehilla, stop pulling that flower! Anyway, like I was saying, I think these prices have really gotten out of hand. And it's not like we could do anything about it. I mean, we can't stop buying baby products, obviously, so we're forced to pay these ridiculous prices! It's a *geneivishe shtick*, I tell you! Don't you agree?" She took a breath and flicked a hair from her *sheitel* out of her heavily mascaraed eyes, waiting for an answer.

Gali looked at the woman, and then, without making a conscious decision about it, she played right along. "Oh, absolutely!" she gushed, waving her hands. "Isn't it just the most ridiculous thing? I mean, really, diapers at these prices; it's pure highway robbery!" She almost started laughing then, but she managed to keep a straight face as the woman nodded self-righteously.

"So how old are your children?" the woman asked Gali, bending over the vegetable display.

Gali's stomach plummeted. *Show's over...* "Oh, excuse me, I must take this call," she stammered, and waving her silent cell phone, she took her cart and spun around as the woman stared open-mouthed after her.

꽁

GALI STRUGGLED WITH THE GROCERY BAGS until she finally found her key, inserted it into the lock, opened the front door — and proceeded to spill a sack of potatoes on the floor. *Oops.*

She scrambled around, collecting the potatoes, and found herself nose to nose with Dovi's shoes. *Huh? That's weird*, she thought. She stuffed the potatoes into one of the bags and got to her feet.

"Dovi?" she called, walking toward the kitchen. "Dovi, are you h— oh!" She stopped short in surprise.

Dovi was sitting at the table with another man she didn't know, both of them clutching coffee cups and looking tense.

Dovi got to his feet. "Gali! I should've told you I'd be home so I could help with the packages! So sorry, here, let me take those..." He hefted the packages out of her limp hands and started to unpack them.

A moment later, he looked up to find his wife shooting daggers at him. "Oh, Gali, this is Avrami Meyers, an old friend of mine. He just moved to Israel. Avrami, my wife."

Gali nodded at the man, realizing that Dovi would probably explain later why he wasn't at second *seder* and why on earth he was having a coffee party with a friend she didn't know. She raised her chin and asked, with impeccable politeness, if she could offer them brownies.

Placing a platter of brownies on the table, she shooed Dovi back to his companion and then began bustling around, putting things away, all the while feeling immensely awkward in her own kitchen. The men, of course, were much quieter with another set of ears around, and they made small talk until Gali announced that she was going to go through her case files and would see Dovi later.

As she walked out of the kitchen, she couldn't help overhearing the beginnings of a heated conversation. She shook her head in confusion. What was that all about? Oh, well; she'd get all the details later on. Right now she needed to focus on her work.

She went into the room she and Dovi used as a joint study and sat down at her desk. She loved this room. With its rustic quaintness, soft rugs, and the two matching, cherry wood, roll-top desks, it resembled something between an old-fashioned library and a coffee shop. She loved to work here at night while Dovi learned quietly at his desk, the two of them whiling away the hours in blissful yet quiet companionship.

But right now there was just her and the stack of case notes in her briefcase. She opened a folder. *Aviva Brach.* Gali sighed. Sometimes she felt far too vulnerable for this job.

September 1, 2015: Patient joins home.

Age: 17

Height: 5'4"

Weight: 90 lb.

Family Situation: Parents separated; sister with serious addiction problem; little brother was killed in a terrorist bombing seven years ago.

Patient Status: Moderate anorexia nervosa. Brought her weight up from 80 lb. at the psychiatric hospital. Came to Healthways for cognitive behavioral therapy.

Counselor Suggested: Family therapy.

Gali snorted. Good luck trying to get Aviva's family to come in for joint therapy sessions. She'd only met Mrs. Brach once, but that had been more than enough. The woman was a whirlwind of loud opinions, disapproval, and quick judgments. Certainly, Gali felt bad for her; after all, she had to be in terrible pain, losing a small child like that.

Though, of course, Gali thought morosely, *I'd first have to know what it's like to* have *a child, before trying to fathom anything else...*

She shook off these self-pitying thoughts and scribbled in the comments section: *Family therapy — good idea, but will take effort... Aviva — hurting, engaging in self-destructive behavior, though medically remains the same.*

She thought back to the cracked lips, translucent skin, and most of all, haunted eyes of the girl she was working with, and she promised herself she would do something about it. She would impact that girl's life for the better. She would.

CHAPTER FOUR

G ali started and gazed around blearily. She must have dozed off over her notes. She squinted at the clock and sat up. She'd been in the study for almost two hours! Dovi couldn't possibly still be talking to that friend of his. She stood up and stretched. Gathering her case files, she slipped them back into their folders, pushed her chair back under the desk, and threw out her empty cup. There, perfect. Gali had decided a while ago that if there were no small, restless hands pulling things out of place, then there was no reason everything shouldn't be set up just so.

She opened the door and was startled to hear voices coming from the kitchen. Dovi was still home, with this Avrami person! Why wasn't he at second *seder*? And what could he possibly be talking about for over two hours with that man? She wasn't one to jump to quick character judgments, but there was something about this Avrami that put her on edge. Or maybe it was just because she had never heard of him before...

She went to her room to change from her *sheitel* and work clothes into something more comfortable. She fixed her snood and then decided to poke her head into the kitchen for a minute, just to check on things.

Now the hallway was quiet. She strode casually into the kitchen and found Dovi sitting at the table, lost in thought. His eyes were glazed over, his forehead a mass of creases, and his hands were resting limply on the glass tabletop. Avrami was nowhere to be seen. She sent up a silent prayer of thanks and cleared her throat.

Dovi jumped and blinked. "Gali! Wow, I didn't hear you come in. How're you doing — you rested at all?" He moved over a seat so she could sit next to him.

She sat down. "Believe it or not, I fell asleep over my notes. So who was that?" She tried to keep the curiosity in her voice to a minimal level.

"Who, Avrami? Oh, the two of us were friendly back in yeshivah high school, although he's a couple of years older than me. Wow, it seems like ages ago..." His voice trailed off.

Gali cleared her throat again.

"Right," Dovi continued. "So we knew each other back then, but then we went our separate ways. He kind of...went in a different direction, if you know what I mean. I think the last time I saw him was sixteen years ago. He looks exactly the same," he mused.

Gali smiled. "So do you," she said. It was true. At thirty-five, Dovi hardly looked any older than how he appeared in their wedding pictures. With his tall frame, sparkling blue eyes, and bright smile, he could have passed for a young man in his early twenties.

Dovi smiled back. "Anyway, so he's divorced now, unfortunately, and he moved to Eretz Yisrael recently for a change of scenery."

Gali stood up and went to the sink to wash the coffee mugs. "So what was with the extremely long and secretive conversation?" she asked.

Dovi looked uncomfortable. "I guess he doesn't really have anyone to talk to. He shared a whole lot more than I wanted to know. He's really hurting..."

Gali turned off the sink, and her heart filled with admiration for her husband's sensitivity. "Invite him for a Shabbos meal," she said impulsively.

"What?" Dovi was taken aback.

Gali picked up another dish, already regretting her invitation. "Sure," she said slowly. "Invite him for Friday night. We're having Mrs. Feldman, of course, and the Schiff twins are here in yeshivah — they're coming with a friend, I think — so why not let him join the fun?"

Gali knew from other members of her infertility support group that Shabbos guests usually dwindled as the empty years dragged on. But that hadn't seemed to happen to them. It was because of Dovi, Gali realized. He was so...comfortable; he made everyone feel welcome. And maybe it was a little bit to her credit, as well.

She turned around to share her thoughts with Dovi, but he was already on the phone. "Hey, Avrami!" he said happily. Gali smiled as he gave her a thumbs-up sign, but inside she felt a sense of foreboding, as if she had just poked a giant hornet's nest. She had the feeling they'd be seeing a lot of Avrami Meyers in the weeks to come.

CHAPTER FIVE

Gali put the finishing touches on her makeup, slipped on her favorite earrings, and switched on the Shabbos lamp in her room before turning off the light. She peeked into the kitchen to make sure the *blech* was working, and then padded into the dining room where Dovi was just finishing to put wicks into her candlesticks.

She gazed at the familiar sight, and something hard and prickly tugged at her heartstrings. She remembered shopping for these candlesticks together with Dovi when they were *chassan* and *kallah* and the joy she had felt every time she opened the candlesticks' box during their engagement. They were so proud and tall, and for those first few years of lighting them, they seemed to fill up the entire room with their glow. But now, years later, they were still standing alone on their tray; they'd never been joined by smaller candlesticks, never been surrounded by homemade, crayon-scribbled *hadlakas neiros* cards. Though the candlesticks were freshly polished, their glow now seemed a tad diminished.

Dovi turned around and smiled at her. "A *gutten Erev Shabbos*," he said, stepping back from the candles.

"A *gutten Erev Shabbos* to you," Gali answered, trying for a light tone. She approached the candles and lit them, then spread her hands and intoned the age-old words that, more than a blessing, were an invitation, a summoning of the holy Shabbos Queen to her home.

As Gali covered her face and *davened*, Dovi stood behind her, his eyes glistening. Then, with a soft, "Good Shabbos," he turned and walked out, as if the sight of his wife's prayers was something too great for him to bear.

"Good Shabbos!" Gali exclaimed, ushering Mrs. Feldman into the living room. At ninety years old, Mrs. Feldman still lived alone. Lately, though, her memory was no longer what it used to be, which had prompted the neighbors on the block to form a rotation among themselves so that Mrs. Feldman would always be with one of them for her Shabbos meals.

Whichever neighbor was to host Mrs. Feldman that week would bring her a card before Shabbos with their name and address written on it so Mrs. Feldman would know exactly where to go.

Now Mrs. Feldman smiled cheerfully at Gali. "Are you" — she peered at her card — "Gali Rothman?" She looked at Gali expectantly.

Gali smiled brightly, though her heart fluttered sadly. Mrs. Feldman had been coming to her for Shabbos for the past three years. For her not to remember Gali showed a serious decline in her condition.

"That's me," she said cheerfully, taking Mrs. Feldman by the arm and leading her to a chair. "Come sit down. The men will be home soon and everything is all ready, so we can schmooze!"

Mrs. Feldman laughed. "I do love to schmooze. If only my David were still here, he would tell you all about it. 'Chatterbox,' he used to call me. We were very happy, you know." She looked at Gali steadily over her glasses. "Married sixty years, and it was a wonderful marriage..."

Gali, who had heard about Mrs. Feldman's late husband myriad times, shook her head sympathetically. "Wow," she said softly. "It must be so hard..."

Mrs. Feldman sighed and smoothed down her plum-colored cardigan. "Oh, it is. But tell me, uh —"

"Gali," Gali supplied.

"Yes, Gali. Are you the hostess?"

Gali froze for a second, and then she recovered. "Yes, good Shabbos. I'm the hostess, Gali Rothman."

"Well, I'm Ruth," Mrs. Feldman said helpfully. "So Gali, do you have any children?"

The smile on Gali's face didn't waver. "No," she said cheerfully. "It's just me and my husband. Do you?" she asked, knowing very well that her guest had three sons, two living in America and one living in Efrat, outside of Yerushalayim.

"Yes, yes, three boys. Nathan, Shaul, and Joshie."

Gali smiled inwardly. "Joshie" was the renowned Rabbi Yehoshua Feldman of a *chashuve* yeshivah in New York.

"And do you have any children?" Mrs. Feldman asked.

Gali blinked. "Um, no, I don't," she said, the cheer in her voice slightly forced this time. "Come," she continued loudly. "Would you like to *daven* together with me?"

Lecha Dodi was a favorite of Mrs. Feldman's, and Gali knew it. The two *davened* together, singing softly, Gali's sweet voice mingling with her older companion's trembling soprano. They finished just as there was a brisk knock at the door, and Dovi walked in, followed by Avrami Meyers.

"Good Shabbos!" Dovi called out.

"Good Shabbos," Gali replied. She smiled coolly at their guest and wished him a polite good Shabbos, too. Closer up, he looked like a man who had been through a lot. His hair was overgrown, his forehead was creased, and he had bags under his eyes, as well as a stubble on his chin that was too scraggly to be there on purpose. She still wasn't a fan of the man, but she did feel bad for him.

"Come in," she said more warmly. "We're still waiting for the three boys, but sit down in the meantime. I'm just going to get the *challos*."

By the time she came out with the two warm *challos* in her hands, the three boys had come, and there were introductions, laughter, and loud talking permeating the room. Gali smiled. She loved hosting.

Dovi clapped Nesanel Schiff on the shoulder, and the two broke out in a hearty "*Shalom Aleichem*." The rest of the men joined in. Gali smiled at Mrs. Feldman, who smiled back.

After Kiddush, Mrs. Feldman leaned in toward Gali. "So tell me..." — she fished around in her pocket for her paper — "Gali. Yes, Gali. Tell me, do you have children?"

Gali tried to stop the heat from flooding her face, but it was to no avail. "N—"

"Mrs. Feldman!" Dovi boomed suddenly, bowing theatrically in their direction. "Can I invite you into the main kitchen for the washing services?"

The old woman tittered. "Why, yes, thank you! Are you my host?" she asked him as he ushered her into the kitchen.

Gali flashed him a silent thank you and sent a silent prayer upward that Mrs. Feldman ask her any question, as many times as she should want, except for this one.

They were just starting the soup when Gavriel Schiff turned to Avrami. "So, you here in yeshivah or something?" he asked him.

Avrami laughed, a hard, brittle sound. "Not so much," he said carelessly. "I'm…doing other stuff. Tried learning a while back, but it wasn't so much my thing. Was the wife's thing, but not mine. Now I figure, no wife, no need for all of that."

He looked up from the salt shaker he was playing with to find all faces at the table wearing expressions of deep discomfort. He laughed again. "Sorry, am I ruining the mood? Don't listen to me." He punched Gavriel's arm. "*Shteig* away, my friend, *shteig* away."

Gali wondered whether she was the only who picked up on the hearty sarcasm in Avrami's voice when he said that or whether it was evident to all. Either way, Mrs. Feldman chose that moment to lean over and ask Avrami if he was the host, and then everything returned to normal.

AFTER THE GUESTS ALL LEFT, the floor was swept, and the food put away, Gali curled up on the couch with a book and a plate of homemade cinnamon buns. She offered one to Dovi, who was settling down at the table with his Chumash. He accepted it and poured a cup of water for her. Peaceful calm reigned in the room, the flickering of the candles lending an ethereal feel to the scene. This was Gali's favorite part of Shabbos. The complete and utter contentment she felt was so real, it was almost tangible.

She sighed happily and flipped a page in her book. She used to buy Jewish weekly magazines, but after years of confronting articles with titles like "Ten Ways to Get Stains Out of Your Little One's Dress," or "How to Know Whether Your Child Has a Behavioral Problem," or "What to Say to Your Neighbor Who Is Battling Infertility," she'd had enough. Now she enjoyed reading full-length Jewish novels, and the occasional biography of a *gadol*.

She was just reaching the climax of the story — the terrorist had entered the building unnoticed! — when Dovi cleared his throat.

She looked up, startled. "Hmm?" she asked, her mind still on her book.

"Gali..."

Something about his voice made the hairs on the back of her neck tingle. "What?" she asked warily, looking up at him.

"Doesn't it bother you?" His hands were twisting the napkin in front of him, his Chumash still open to the first *perek*.

"Doesn't what bother me, Dovi?"

"Our efforts!" The words burst out angrily, and she blinked.

"What?" she asked again. "What efforts?"

"Ours!" he said loudly. "Here we are, week after week, being good, kind Jews. We invite guests to our table — old ladies, divorced men, hungry *yeshivah bachurim*. We *daven*, we learn, we're very *makpid* on halachah... Where's our reward? Where's the fairness? Every day we give our all to Hashem, and the one thing we really want, we can't have. It...it just bothers me!" He looked at Gali, at the utter horror that was evident on every inch of her face, and his fire burned out.

"Oh, Gali, forget it. Forget I said anything. I think...I just need to sleep. Good Shabbos. Thank you for the beautiful *seudah*." And just like that, he closed his Chumash, kissed it gently, and headed off to bed.

If he would have turned around, he would have seen his wife staring after him, her mouth still slightly open in shock, and two Shabbos candles that seemed to glow a little less in the wake of his tirade.

CHAPTER SIX

She gazed steadily at the girl sitting across from her. The girl stared back for a moment, and then dropped her eyes. Gali waited for her to speak first.

Another minute went by and then, "It is not my fault."

Gali smiled inwardly — awkward silence worked almost every time — and then replied calmly, "What's not your fault, Natalia?"

The daughter of Russian immigrants, Natalia had lived in New York for most of her seventeen years before making *aliyah* to Israel with her family two years back. She conversed in a mixture of broken Hebrew sprinkled with English, so she'd been assigned to Gali, who was fluent in both languages.

Gali studied Natalia. The girl would have been beautiful if it weren't for her illness. She had large, doe-shaped brown eyes, blond hair that she pulled into a low bun, both of these accenting her unusually high cheekbones... But now the look was marred by the dullness of her brown eyes, the cracks in her blond hair, and the fact that her cheekbones were now so sharp, they could probably cut glass. The wastefulness of it all tore Gali's insides to pieces, as it always did when she thought about it, but she determinedly pushed her own thoughts and feelings to the side.

"The weight loss," Natalia answered finally.

Gali didn't blink. "And why do you think that is?" she asked, purposely not specifying her question.

"Well, I think it is my mother's fault that I lost the weight. She doesn't have supper on time, and I cannot eat so late. Going to sleep full makes me feel bloated and heavy."

Gali sighed. The Gavrikovs had promised the Healthways counselor that they would abide by the strict "family dinner" rule if they wanted Natalia to remain an outpatient. Apparently, the plan wasn't really working.

"And why do you think it is hard for your mother to have dinner on the table by six thirty?" she asked casually.

Natalia blushed. "Well, that is when she..." The rest of the sentence was lost in an incoherent mumble.

Gali leaned forward. "I'm sorry, what was that?" she asked.

"I said, that is when she exercises." Natalia's blush deepened, proving that she realized just how ridiculous this was.

Gali felt the anger rise up within her, and she forced herself to stay calm. "I see," was all she said. "Natalia, I'd like you to go join group therapy now, please. And when would be the best time to call your mother?" she asked, escorting the girl out of her office.

Wouldn't want to interrupt her workout, she added silently, rolling her eyes.

Her next appointment of the day wasn't scheduled for another twenty minutes, so she decided to go grab a coffee and banana from the kitchen. She scanned her schedule as she walked. *11:45 a.m....* *Aviva*. Gali hadn't realized her next appointment was with her. She felt her pulse race inexplicably. It was going to be a hard session.

Aviva had not gained the desired weight that week, and Gali had to do her best to change that. Healthways's policy was that there was no point in therapy if the patient was still starving, so they emphasized weight gain strongly for the patient's first few months there, and once the numbers were okay, the staff moved on to ensuring that the mind be where the body was at. Though Aviva had been an inpatient for more than a few months, her weight was still fluctuating. Gali sighed. She'd better go get that coffee; she was going to need it.

The kitchen was mostly empty. A small table in the corner was occupied by three of her coworkers, including Chedva, another social worker. Gali smiled. She really liked Chedva. She went to pour herself some brewed French vanilla, and then walked over to the table slowly, trying not to spill.

"And then he said, 'Mommy, I'm still hun—' Oh, hi, Gali!" The three women stopped chattering immediately and looked uncomfortable.

Gali was used to it. "Oh my gosh, Chedva, did Tzviki wake you up *again* for cholent?" she asked breezily, settling herself down at the table and flipping her *sheitel* over one shoulder.

Chedva laughed. "Nope, this time it was for matzah!" Everyone laughed, and the tension was broken.

Gali cut up her banana neatly, and ate it in between sips of coffee. "Mmm." She sighed. "Oh, Rachel, I wanted to ask you for the recipe for your coffee marble cake. I'll call you later, okay?"

"Sure," Rachel said quietly.

Gali knew her childlessness made Rachel uneasy, and she resolved to do something about it. Maybe they should go out for lunch one day or something. In the meantime, she had to run to her session with Aviva. She murmured a *brachah acharonah*, said goodbye to the women, and hurried out.

She stood outside the light pink door once again, her heart thumping. "Please, Hashem," she *davened*, "please put the right words in my mouth to help heal this young girl. Please, *Hakadosh Baruch Hu*, science and medicine and psychology are nothing except Your tools. Please help me help her…" Gali stood there for another minute and then knocked lightly on the door.

"Aviva?" she called quietly.

The door opened, and there she was. Gali shifted into social worker gear. "Good afternoon," she said brightly, mentally taking notes on her client's appearance. Aviva appeared weak, but not frail; pale, but not ghost-like. It could have been worse. "So, would you like to talk in your room, or shall we head to the lounge?" Gali asked.

"Lounge," Aviva muttered, brushing past Gali and stalking off in that direction. Gali just barely refrained from rolling her eyes and followed calmly after the girl. She found her slumped in a large, overstuffed, mustard-colored armchair. Against the yellow, Aviva really did look white.

Gali settled into a paisley love seat right across from her. She leaned back casually. "So, Aviva, how are you?"

Aviva glared at her. "Oh, I'm *amazing*. No, really, I'm having a buh-*last*. Oh, please, don't make me leave! I want to stay forever!"

Gali blinked at the overdose of sarcasm. She really hated sarcasm, come to think of it. She decided to play along. "Well, that's fantastic, Aviva! I'm so glad you're enjoying. You know, I always say that if done right, therapy can be fun, as well as useful! Good for you, Aviva, good for you!" She smiled sweetly.

Aviva glared even harder. "Whatever," she said, reverting back to sullen teenager.

Gali smiled to herself. "Anyway, Aviva, I'd like to know why your weight has gone down this week."

Aviva shrugged and pulled her sleeve over her fist protectively. "Dunno," she said.

Gali leaned toward her. "Aviva, can you please try to figure it out?"

The girl shrugged again. "I really don't know! I eat everything I'm supposed to, and I even exercised less this week."

Gali gazed at her. She seemed to be telling the truth. "Well, then, do you know what this means? I'm pretty sure your body is trying to tell us that it needs more fuel to keep going. This is a good thing, Aviva!" She smiled at the girl, who looked utterly horrified.

"More food? Are you out of your mind? No way! I refuse!" Aviva said vehemently. "Don't you dare try to force-feed me!"

Gali let her blow off some steam before breaking in. "*Chas v'shalom*, Aviva, no one will force-feed you. And I'm not talking about much, just one additional yogurt per day."

Aviva gasped. "That's 250 calories! No way!" she shouted, sudden panic streaking across her face.

Gali reached out and touched her arm. "Aviva?"

The girl looked at her, tears spilling over her lashes.

Gali swallowed. "Did anyone ever tell you that you have beautiful eyes?" she asked suddenly, and then Aviva's tears fell, and she let them.

For half an hour, Aviva sat there, gasping and shuddering, until her flow of tears ran dry. And when the tears stopped, the girl's words filled their place. "No," Aviva whispered.

Gali just looked at her.

"No, no one ever told me I have beautiful eyes. They told me I was fat. They told me I had crooked teeth, that my clothes were out of style. They pointed out the acne and the freckles. But never my eyes. And then I got the braces, the skin care, and I went on a diet. And for one glorious year, I was popular, I was pretty, I was 'in.' And then my mother put me in *here*! Right when I was so close to having forgotten everything, all my hard times. Now everyone's trying to make me go back to what I was. I was a *nothing*, do you understand?"

She paused and looked at Gali. "No, of course you don't understand. How could you? How could you know what it's like not to fit in, to feel like a huge elephant in the middle of a pack of beautiful deer? You're just so..." Her voice trailed off spitefully, and she wiped her eyes.

Impulsively, Gali decided to finish her sentence. "Childless," she said.

Aviva looked up, shocked out of her one-person pity party. "What?"

Gali smiled. "You were saying what I am, so I thought I would help you out. I'm childless. Pretty, yes. Thin, yes. An elephant amidst deer? Maybe not. But a deer amidst elephants is just as lonely and afraid. Think about it." And with those parting words, she patted Aviva softly on the arm, gathered her papers, and headed off to her next appointment.

CHAPTER SEVEN

She practically ran home from the bus stop. She was late; Dovi would be home in an hour. Their long-standing tradition of going out for waffles once a month often coincided with her late hours, and she usually found herself rushing like crazy in order to make it. But it was worth everything.

The two of them had agreed long ago that as long as they were sitting in their favorite booth, and the table in front of them was laden with things like steaming waffles, mounds of whipped cream, and sliced fruit, there was to be no talk of sadness or pain. They both looked forward eagerly to these "dates," and Gali tried to wear something different or dressy to them. Tonight she planned to wear the new sweater she had bought last week. It was a muted gold, and the threads in it seemed to glow in different shades, depending on the lighting. She loved it and was excited for its debut.

It was funny, she mused. At times like this, she didn't feel the usual emptiness. She felt thirteen years younger, like she was the same nervous post-seminary girl waiting for her date to arrive at her parents' home. She smiled to herself. It was definitely one of the silver linings to their situation: she and Dovi were probably as close as a couple could possibly get. They could finish each other's unspoken sentences, let alone the ones that were said aloud. Lately, of course, Dovi had been acting strangely, but now was not the time to dwell on that.

She unlocked the front door, slammed it behind her, and raced to her room. Forty minutes later, she emerged, feeling beautiful. She wore her Shabbos *sheitel*, its dark, glossy locks falling in delicate waves. Diamond studs — a ten-year anniversary present from Dovi — glistened in her earlobes, matching the pendant around her neck. She'd matched the gold sweater with a suede, forest-green skirt, and brown leather ballet flats completed the look.

She went to grab a game from the hallway closet. Sometimes there was a wait at the café, and the two of them liked to play something while they waited. She chose Balderdash and slipped it into her handbag.

The door opened, and Dovi sashayed inside, holding a bouquet of champagne-colored daisies, her favorite.

"Awww," she said shyly. "Thank you! I love this kind of flower!"

"I know," he said, and they both laughed. She went to put them in a vase, and then met Dovi by the door.

"Shall we?" he asked, holding the door open for her.

"We shall," she said, bobbing her head royally, and they walked out into the Jerusalem evening, giggling like schoolchildren.

"OH MY GOSH, DOVI, I can't believe I let you talk me into this!" Gali said as the waitress slid a towering pile of pancakes in front of them.

Dovi laughed gleefully. "It said 'The Pancake Challenge.' Now how was I supposed to pass that up?"

Gali giggled. "Yeah, the challenge is getting out of bed in the morning after you've eaten forty pancakes!"

Dovi picked up a fork. "Well, challenge accepted! Come on, we can always bring home the leftovers in a doggy bag or something. Let's eat!"

Gali eyed the tower and then slipped a golden, chocolate-chip-studded circle onto her plate. "Mmm..." She sighed. "This is *so* good!" Dovi smiled at her, and she suddenly felt self-conscious.

"What?" she asked, putting down her fork.

"Nothing!" Dovi said quickly. "I just like to see you...happy."

Gali blushed. "Well, I'm not a big fan of seeing you down, either," she said teasingly.

He lifted his fork high in the air, a blueberry stuck on one prong. "Here's to happy spouses!"

Gali lifted her chocolate milkshake. "To happy spouses!" she agreed with a laugh, and then they proceeded to play a spirited round of Balderdash.

❧

THE NIGHT WAS COOL as they walked home, the scent of pine wafting through the air and the taste of maple syrup in their mouths.

"I messed up today," Gali said suddenly.

"I highly doubt that," Dovi said, lazily.

"No, Dovs, I did. A client was sharing, and I shared back. I got way too personal, telling her about *my* life and *my* feelings. What was I thinking?"

Dovi was silent. Gali looked at him, but his eyes were dark. Finally, he said, "It's what you do, Gals. You give and give, selflessly. You give of your whole self, and silly social worker etiquette wasn't going to stand in your way."

They arrived at their apartment. Gali gave him a half-smile. "Thanks for tonight," she said, following him inside.

"Thank *you*," he said.

And the door closed behind them as they entered their silent home.

CHAPTER EIGHT

Gali fingered her cell phone thoughtfully. Healthways had just called to say that they needed her to come in on Tuesday for a meeting, so she could have today off instead. Tuesday was her standard day off, and she usually did all of her errands then, but maybe she could switch around her schedule... Yes, she could definitely make it work. She called back Mrs. Rappaport, and it was all settled.

So what to do now? Should she go back to sleep? Or maybe she should treat herself and pick up breakfast from somewhere nice, maybe Green's in Rechavia? Decisions, decisions.

She decided to sleep for a little bit more, and then head out to do some shopping and maybe take a trip to the Kosel. Her plans made for the day, she snuggled under her covers, still dressed, and fell back asleep.

An hour later, she sat up with a start. Someone was moving around in the apartment. She was sure of it.

Immediately, she panicked. Who could it be? And how could the person have gotten in? The front door had been locked; Dovi always locked the door behind himself when he left the house in the morning. Someone had broken into her home!

Oh, no, oh, no, Hashem, please, please, don't let it be Arab terrorists! she prayed. *Please let it just be some bored teenager looking for a laptop or something!*

She sat there, frozen in fear, clutching her cell phone with hands that were slippery with sweat. Should she call the police? What was their number again? Was it 900? Or 100? *Omigosh*, she thought frantically. *I don't even know the police's number!* This could not be happening.

And then, before she could do anything, the bedroom door started to open. She wildly grabbed at the bedside lamp with both hands... and Dovi walked in.

She shrieked. "Dovi! You scared the living daylights out of me! I was going to call the police! Oh...my...gosh!" The realization and relief that she wasn't going to be a tragic story on the news began to sink in, and she buried her face in a pillow, sobbing quietly.

Dovi stood in the doorway, looking like the proverbial deer caught in the headlights. He looked at his crying wife. "What?" he asked dumbly.

Gali looked up, her carefully applied eye makeup from that morning now gray streaks on her face, and she started to laugh hysterically.

Dovi smiled tentatively, not exactly sure what had just happened, and not sure if he was still to blame. Gali caught sight of his face, and that just caused her to laugh harder.

"What?" he asked again. "Are you...feeling okay?"

"Thought — you — were — terrorists!" Gali finally choked out.

"Oh," he said, the events now taking shape in his mind. "Now I get it! Oh, I'm so sorry! And you, Gali, must stop reading those action novels!" he added. He walked hesitantly across the room, still seeming unsure if she would knock him out with the lamp in her hands.

Gali sighed, put the lamp down, and sat primly on her bed, wiping her eyes. "Whew!" she exhaled, trying to calm herself. "That was crazy."

Dovi poured a cup of water for her from the bottle on the nightstand. "Yeah... So, why are you home now, besides for trying to catch terrorists?"

Gali giggled, made a *brachah*, and took a sip. "Thanks. Oh, I'm home because Healthways switched my day off for this week. Thought I'd sleep in a little. Wait, why are *you* home now? Are you not feeling well?" she asked, her voice sharp with concern.

Dovi blushed. "No, I feel fine, *baruch Hashem*. I just...needed a little break..." His voice trailed off. Gali looked at him trustingly as he continued. "I, um, I told the yeshivah I needed a few days..."

Gali stared at him, trying to understand. Dovi was the itinerary coordinator and unofficial life coach for the *shanah aleph* boys in his old yeshivah. He then learned with the *rosh yeshivah* during second *seder*. It was an arrangement he usually loved, and he often marveled at how, even after twelve years of marriage, he was still learning in *kollel*. His paycheck wasn't that much, of course, but together with the salary Gali received from Healthways and Gali's parents' generous gifts, there was always considerably more than enough to go around.

"You need a break?" she asked slowly, not sure what it was that was causing her voice to come out harsher than she intended. She tried to soften her tone. "Was it getting to be too much, being in yeshivah all day?"

"No..." Dovi walked over to the window and stood there, his back to his wife, gazing out at the Jerusalem street below him. He watched an old man wheel a green cart full of groceries past the front of their house. He followed the man's progress until he was out of sight, and then he spoke quickly. "It's just that...how can I talk to these boys, reassure them, guide them...if I, myself, feel lost?" He turned to face her, and Gali was startled by the tears on her strong, stoic husband's face.

"Dovi?" she said uncertainly. She suddenly noticed the pain etched into his normally relaxed features, pain she'd never seen there before.

He sat down on his bed. "I'm lost, Gali," he said quietly, his voice cracking. "I don't know how, but suddenly, I'm unsure of everything. I have trouble with the most basic, simple concepts of *emunah*. I feel...like I woke up one morning, and everything is different. Like I'm in the same bed, but in a different country, with a different language, one that I can't comprehend. The only thing I do know..." He looked at her as he spoke. "The only thing I do know is that I'm going to need you by my side, helping me through all this. Will you be there for me, Gali? Will you be there, even if it gets rough?" He lifted his chin, unashamed of his plea.

Gali sat there for a minute, wondering how everything had changed so suddenly, but her heart was quicker than her mind, and it was with this that she answered him. "I'll be there, Dovi. We're a team. You've been there for me these past twelve years; now it's my turn. I promise you" — her voice was firm — "I'll always be at your side."

The two sat there silently, on opposite sides of a room that suddenly seemed miles long, and the sun rose higher in the sky as the tears dried slowly on the young man's face.

CHAPTER NINE

Nothing really changed in the Rothman home, yet somehow, everything was different. Suddenly, Dovi was doing the grocery shopping, cooking, and baking. He started playing the flute again — something he hadn't done since he was a teenager — and Gali was constantly tripping over its case or accidentally making grocery lists on the back of his sheet music. Sometimes she'd fall asleep at night in an empty room, with haunting melodies wafting their way into her dreams. Dovi still learned second *seder* with Rabbi Gordon, the *rosh yeshivah*, but even that was different. He used to walk in afterward glowing from the inside, like one of those lanterns Gali used to decorate the sukkah. Now he came home almost angrily, greeted Gali, and practically ran toward his flute.

It hurt her to see her husband in pain, but there didn't seem to be anything she could do about it. He would brush off her attempts at *hashkafah* conversations, and he would practically roll his eyes if she put too much enthusiasm into her own *avodas Hashem*. He was now enrolled in a cooking class along with none other than Avrami Meyers. Gali's teeth clenched just at the sound of the man's name. She blamed him for Dovi's confusion, though she knew it couldn't have been completely his fault. But she was positive he did have a big hand in Dovi changing, and she did not, would not, forgive him for that.

Her problems weren't only on the home front. At Healthways, she was also experiencing frustration. Progress with Aviva had seemed to plateau after their heart-to-heart in the lounge. The girl was no longer bitingly aggressive, but she was now passively antagonistic, which Gali found to be extremely irksome. She was eating more, but she seemed to have taken a vow of silence during therapy, refusing to utter a word to Gali.

Gali sighed as she walked into a nearby café after work one day. If there was ever a time for an iced caramel latte with whipped cream, this was it. She pulled off her sunglasses, squinting as her eyes adjusted to the dimmer lighting in the café.

"No! Gali Lerner?!"

Gali spun around, feeling slightly disoriented. "Chaviva?" she gasped.

Chaviva Hellman had been Miss Popular in high school. Small, blond, and petite, she had been dance head, *chessed* head, and Shabbaton head, and was privately voted in as the girl most likely to get married straight out of seminary. She had, of course, and after that, Gali had lost track of her. Now here she was, slightly plumper, but just as pretty, wearing an emerald-colored chenille snood that made her green eyes sparkle. She was surrounded by four small blond children, all licking ice cream cones.

Chaviva laughed. "Wow, blast from the past! How *are* you, Gali? Do you live here? What are you up to? Oh my gosh, let's sit!"

That was how Gali found herself sitting in a booth in a café in Rechavia, looking across at her former dance head.

"So we're just visiting. My husband had a work conference in Yerushalayim this week and was coming in, so we decided to come along with him. Ruchie's bas mitzvah is coming up, so we're taking her to Kever Rochel, and the rest of the kids are just enjoying being on vacation here. I mean, I know they're missing a week of school, but it's worth it, you know?" She rolled her green eyes dramatically and laughed.

"So how about you, Gali? I can't believe I don't even know who you married!"

Gali laughed politely. "Dovi Rothman," she said, smiling. "I feel like I'm engaged again — do you want to see my ring?" she quipped, and the two laughed. Gali excused herself to go pick up her drink, and then returned, licking whipped cream off the rim of the cup.

Chaviva sighed when she saw that. "Yu-um. I don't know how you stay so thin. I feel like every time I leave the hospital with one of my cuties, I take home a bigger dress size! Oh well, worth the exchange, right?" she said with a wink, leaning over to wipe chocolate syrup off her little girl's face.

Gali thought about lying, but she was so tired of playing games; Aviva's cat-and-mouse techniques had thoroughly depleted her. "I wouldn't know," she said quietly, taking a long sip of her iced coffee.

She looked up to find Chaviva staring at her, tears sparkling in her large eyes. Gali felt horrible. "Oh no," she said hurriedly. "It's okay, really! I mean, you know, I wish things were different and that we did have kids, but it's been so many years and..."

Her words were lost as Chaviva walked around the table. Suddenly, Gali found herself in the embrace of a girl she hadn't seen in thirteen years. She closed her eyes, enjoying the feeling of another's caring.

❧

SHE WALKED INTO HER APARTMENT a few hours later, laden down with shopping bags. *Nothing like a little retail therapy to get your mind off your problems*, she thought, envisioning the new pair of earrings she had just purchased. She began to lay out her new things on the couch to show Dovi when he got home.

Just then, her cell phone rang. She looked at the screen, frowning at the unfamiliar number.

She picked it up. "Hello?"

The voice sounded a bit hesitant. "Hi, Gali, it's Chaviva. I...I wanted to ask you something..."

❧

DOVI WALKED IN, whistling a cheerful tune. He was happy that he felt good today; he disliked coming home in his all-too-frequent haze of confusion. He felt terrible bringing that home to Gali.

"Hello!" he called cheerfully, peeking into the kitchen. It was empty. He turned and walked toward the living room. There was Gali, sitting on the couch with her head in her hands, surrounded by shopping bags.

Dovi smiled at the sight of the bags. He loved when Gali treated herself to a shopping trip. Though she came from a financially comfortable family, Gali was far from spoiled. She refused to let Dovi buy a car, claiming that if the bus and light rail were good enough for everyone else in their neighborhood, then they were good enough for the two of them, too. They rarely went on expensive vacations, preferring instead to plumb the depths of the holy country they lived in. But every now and then, Gali got the shopping bug, and it made Dovi feel good when she gave in to it. She deserved whatever pleasure she could get in life, especially now that he was burdening her with so many new problems...

"Shopping, hmm?" he asked cheerily, going to sit next to her on the leather couch. Gali didn't move.

"Gali?" Now his tone was uncertain. "Are you okay?"

She picked up her head, and he caught a glimpse of something he hadn't seen in her for years now. It was hope, pure and simple.

Dovi did not allow himself to get excited. He just waited for her to speak.

"Dovi," Gali said huskily. "I got a phone call from an old friend of mine, Chaviva Hellman..." She swallowed, and wiped her hands nervously on her skirt. "Her sister Shoshana, who lives in Eretz Yisrael, just had a baby, but she is suffering from a recurring case of severe postpartum depression. She has six other children that the family needs to take care of, and they are looking for someone to care for the baby for a few months...and she thought of me."

Dovi stared at her, his mouth slack. "What?" he asked, his mind trying to comprehend what was occurring.

"A baby, Dovi! They want us to take in a baby!" Gali's voice rose, and that last word echoed around the room. A baby.

Chapter Ten

A baby. She wanted to foster a baby.

He laughed derisively and kicked a rock. He could barely put one foot in front of the other without falling down, and she wanted to take in someone else's baby. He ran his fingers through his hair and held on for a moment, feeling the strain at the roots and enjoying the pressure. He had to hold on to something, anything, before he exploded.

He looked around at the kids playing, the men on their phones, and the women chatting with friends, hands perched casually on the strollers in front of them, and he wondered how they all appeared so *normal*. Was it just him? Was he the only one who couldn't handle life, who couldn't play the role he was given? Was he the only one messing up his lines so badly that he didn't recognize the man who looked back at him from the mirror?

His phone rang. He glanced at the screen and gave a wry smile. Misery sure loved company. Avrami Meyers was doing pretty badly too. The thought was comforting, and he pressed the "talk" button.

"Where you at, Rothman?"

Dovi smirked. "Oh, you know, *shteiging*. Just came up with such a brilliant *pshat*, they've named me *gadol hador*."

Avrami snickered. "That doesn't say a lot about our *dor*, Dovs."

Dovi felt a deep sadness at those words, and suddenly he was tired of games, of jokes. "I'm in the park. What's up?"

Avrami sounded bored. "Cooking class for today is being rescheduled. Big Mike has a wedding or something."

Big Mike was their cooking teacher, and a master chef himself. He got his name from brushing seven feet and being almost as wide. He looked more like a linebacker than a chef, but his cooking was really something else.

Dovi sighed. There went that distraction. "Wanna do something else together, then?" he asked Avrami, looking around again at the pleasant scenery surrounding him. Everyone else seemed so purposeful; even relaxing at a park seemed to hold meaning for them all. But there he was, as aimless as a three-year-old, wandering the path with nowhere to go.

"Well, there's this thing in Tel Aviv," Avrami said slowly.

Dovi tensed. When Avrami said "thing" and "Tel Aviv" in the same sentence, it did not sound good. "You know that's not my scene," he said steadily.

Avrami snorted. "Oh, please, I know my *yeshivah bachur* friend better than that. Nah, it's a class on how to cook with wine — very up and up, don't worry."

Dovi thought about it. Gali was at the clinic, probably making lists of everything they needed for the baby — she'd probably painted the guest room already! — and all of his friends were either at work or in *kollel*, so...

"Sounds good," he said. He hung up and looked around the park one more time. Then, quickly, before he changed his mind, he took off at a brisk pace for the Central Bus Station.

≈

"So, by 'how to cook with wine,' you meant wine tasting?" Dovi asked Avrami, half-annoyed and half-amused, a sentiment he felt often when in the presence of Avrami Meyers.

Meyers laughed. "Well, yeah. You know, tasting the wine will help us know which wines are good with which meats... It'll come in handy cooking-wise, believe me."

Dovi sighed. "At least the wine here has a good *hechsher*," he grumbled, rubbing his forehead.

"So what's got you all stressed out?" Avrami asked as they accepted cups of a deep burgundy merlot. Dovi made a *brachah* and took a sip. Avrami just took a sip.

Dovi closed his eyes. "My wife wants to take in a foster baby," he said, a pained expression coming over his face.

Avrami stopped swirling his cup. "Are you serious?" he asked incredulously.

"You bet," Dovi said, trying to keep the bitterness in his voice to a minimum.

"Yeesh," Avrami said. He shook his head in sympathy. "I mean, I love my kids, but don't ask me to wake up at 2:00 a.m. for a kid who isn't mine!"

Dovi just stared at his glass, trying not to let his anger get the better of him. He wasn't even sure whom he was angry at. Well, Gali, to start with. Not at her, of course, just, well, at her. *Argh!* He groaned out loud and dropped his head onto the bar.

"Boy or girl?" Avrami asked, glancing down at his friend with an amused expression on his face.

"Boy," Dovi said hoarsely. He banged his head against the cool marble. Then he sat up suddenly and looked at Avrami. "Twelve years," he said softly. "Twelve years I've waited for us to have a baby of our own. I can wait. This? This is a cop-out. Oh, we can't have our own baby? Great, let's borrow someone else's! Grab a cup of sugar while you're at it!" He picked up his glass and downed its contents in one gulp. Then he reached for Avrami's.

"Hey," his friend protested as Dovi gulped down his wine.

"You snooze, you lose," Dovi mumbled, wiping his mouth on the back of his hand. "And the best part? Gali's going back to work after two weeks! So you know who's going to be the stay-at-home daddy?!"

His voice was getting louder. He knew he was drunk, but he didn't care. Avrami was staring at him like he'd never seen him before. "Me, that's who! Good ol' Dovi, with no job, no normal learning schedule, no life! Might as well change diapers and give baths! Hey, maybe I can just start a nursery!" Avrami tried to put a hand on his shoulder, but Dovi shoved him off. "What has my life become, Meyers? What have I become?" he moaned.

Avrami took Dovi by the shoulders and gave him a little shake. "Dovi, snap out of it. This is all eye-opening for you! You weren't happy all along, but you just never knew it. Now you do! You might say that this revelation you're having is the best thing that has ever happened to you!"

But Dovi wasn't listening; he was too focused on trying to make the room stop spinning.

"Come," Avrami said, inserting a hand under Dovi's elbow and half-carrying him out of the bar. "Let's go help you forget all about your troubles."

&

DOVI TIPTOED INTO THE HOUSE several hours later, trying not to make noise. He grabbed at the lamp as it threatened to fall over and knocked over the decorative bowl full of pinecones that Gali had on the side table. They scattered, and he bent to pick them up before Gali came out and —

"Dovi?" The voice was sleepy, but she was definitely up.

"Hey, Gals," he called out, hoping he sounded normal and not as hung over as he felt, after spending the night out on the town, bar-hopping.

"Hey, how are you? Should I come make you some tea for your headache?"

He'd texted Gali from the bus that cooking class was running late and that he'd be home soon, but with a splitting headache. If she was surprised that his class had ended at eleven o'clock at night, she didn't say anything.

Dovi felt a sharp stab of pain; he never used to lie to his wife. "No, that's okay. Please, go back to sleep. I'll be there in five minutes."

"'Kay, goodnight," she mumbled, and then it was quiet once more.

He went into the bathroom and stared at his reflection. His eyes were bloodshot, his skin looked old, and his hair was mussed and greasy. He honestly had never seen himself look so bad in all his thirty-five years.

"This is what you look like after partying like a bum," he told himself. "It's not pretty."

His reflection looked back at him mournfully. He gave the mirror a little salute and then turned to take a long, hot shower.

ع

OF COURSE HE NOTICED. Rabbi Gordon noticed *everything*.

Dovi sighed and opened his front door wider. "Rebbi, what an honor! Come on in. Can I get you a drink?"

Rabbi Gordon smiled at the uncomfortable young man before him. Clearly this was an "honor" Dovi would have been happy to do without. "I'm alright, Dovi, thank you." He followed his host into the living room and settled himself on a chair. Dovi sat down opposite him.

For a moment, both men were silent. Then Rabbi Gordon spoke. "Dovi," he said softly.

Dovi just looked at him.

"Dovi," he said again.

Dovi's eyes dropped to the floor. "Please...please don't," he finally mumbled.

"Don't what?" Rabbi Gordon asked kindly.

"Please don't say my name like that," Dovi said hoarsely.

"Like what?"

"Like...like you love me," Dovi answered brokenly. And then he was crying, crying like he hadn't in months, in years, even, the sobs escaping from his mouth, from his heart, from his soul.

"I'm broken," he cried. "There's nothing left to love, Rebbi."

Rabbi Gordon watched him, a tear of his own sliding down his face. "You know that's not true, Dovi'le. There's always what to love. And nothing is more whole than a broken heart. I came to tell you how much I — we all — miss you in yeshivah. Come back, Dovi. I'll help you. Come back to yeshivah, and you'll see how alive, how *whole*, you can feel."

Dovi choked. "I can't, Rebbi. I'm too far. And please don't tell me that a Jew is never too far or anything like that. I can't. I don't want to talk about it. I don't want help. Just let me fall, Rebbi. I need my space. I need...I need to fall," he finished quietly.

Rabbi Gordon looked penetratingly at him. "I'll give you space, Dovi," he finally said. "But not so you can fall. I'll give you space so that you can make your own way home again." He stood up and walked to the door. Then he stopped.

"And you will, *b'ezras Hashem*. I have confidence in you, Dovi. And always remember that I'm here for you."

A moment later he was gone.

CHAPTER ELEVEN

The air was filled with promises, like the scent of summer on a winter day. Gali inhaled, and then let out her breath in a silent whoosh. She ran her hand over her *sheitel*, smoothed her coat, and lifted her chin. She gazed silently at the storefront before her. It had large neon letters proudly proclaiming its name to the entire street: "Best Baby."

She remembered a younger version of herself, a less jaded one, who used to walk into this store with confidence to exclaim over the tiny booties and pretty crib sets, certain that her day would come to actually purchase them. But as that day had never arrived, her visits had stopped. She hadn't entered a baby store in over six years. She felt like an imposter — but that wasn't going to stop her. Nothing was going to stop her, not here, not today. Not even Dovi's gentle but firm refusal to join her.

He had thought the whole idea was a bad one. "Just think how empty we'll feel when he leaves," he'd begged Gali.

She had looked at him, eyes sparkling with joy. "But think how full we'll feel when he's here!" she'd reiterated. And that was that.

She stepped inside. "Ooh!" she exclaimed aloud. Cribs were set up strategically on the main floor, each one resplendent with adorable linen and mobiles. Stacks of cozy blankets were piled on dresser tops; little hats were hanging from hooks. Baby bathtubs, bassinets, and car seats were on display, different models all vying for attention. Gali swallowed and felt the tears pricking at her eyelids. So long. She had waited so long to buy something miniature-sized, something, anything that spoke of fragility and newness. And here she was, at last... and it wasn't even for her own baby.

She glanced around at the other women in the store. Some were pushing strollers casually in front of them; some were obviously expecting; and some were, no doubt, *kvelling* bubbies. Well, she was going to be a foster mother, and that was real, too, she thought with a surge of defiance.

"Excuse me," she called to a passing saleswoman. "What's the best bassinet for a four-week-old?"

"Ah, mazel tov!" the lady exclaimed, eyeing Gali's slender figure askance.

Gali smiled at this. "Thank you," she said, nodding regally. She followed the woman to the bassinets. There were big ones and small ones, wooden ones and plastic ones. They came in white, brown, pink, blue, black... Gali felt her heart swell. Her hands twitched, aching to hold the child she never had.

The woman was listing the merits of each bassinet, but Gali wasn't listening. She'd found the one she wanted. It was made of cream-colored wood and resembled a tall cradle. It was being shown with a cream and light blue chevron-patterned sheet and a matching fleece blanket. Hanging from the bassinet was a mobile from which sheep with blue ribbons around their necks danced in a circle.

"I'll take this one!" she announced, interrupting the detailed sales pitch. "With the linen, the mobile...the whole thing!"

The woman blinked. "This is a very well-made piece. It's quite high-end, you realize."

Gali smiled. For once, she was going to buy something extravagant. "That's just fine," she answered, already picturing the beautiful bassinet set up in their guest room. "It's just fine with me."

ෂ

"Dovi?" Gali entered the apartment, her arms full of packages. There was no answer, but she heard the sound of music coming from their bedroom. She dropped the bags on the couch and walked toward their room. "Knock-knock?" she called through the door.

The music stopped abruptly. Gali's forehead wrinkled. Had that been...the radio?

The door opened, and Dovi stood there, his face flushed. "Hi!" he said. "I didn't hear you come in. How was it?"

She gazed at him for a moment and then decided to ignore the music. "It was...unreal," she said, lowering her eyes to the floor.

Dovi smiled. "I'm glad. I'm sorry I didn't come with you, Gali. It's just...I wanted..."

"I know," she broke in. "Me too. You wanted it to be for *our* baby..."

They were quiet for a moment, and then Gali decided it was time for a conducive cheer-up. "Wanna see what I got?" she asked brightly.

Dovi looked relieved and answered in the same tone, "Sure!" He followed her out of the room and sat down on the recliner in the living room, kicking up the footrest and leaning all the way back.

Gali giggled at his ultra-relaxed pose and sat down among her bags. "Okay, first of all, look at this. Just look at how teeny-weeny this is!" She held up a package of three undershirts, one butter-yellow, one white, and one powder-blue. "And look at these!" She held up a pair of suede booties. "And this!" She held up a tiny knit hat.

Dovi was cracking up at her excitement, and Gali felt a rush of contentment, of rightness. Wasn't this exactly how it was supposed to be? Light spilling into her home…a laughing, happy husband…baby paraphernalia littering her couch… She closed her eyes and took a mental picture, freezing the moment for a rainy day. Then she blinked; Dovi had been speaking.

"Sorry, what'd you say?" she asked.

"I said, aren't you going to get ready? It's almost time to go."

Gali stared at him. "Go?" she repeated blankly. "Go where?"

Now it was Dovi's turn to stare. "Um, to your cousin's wedding?"

Gali looked stricken. "Oh my goodness! Michoel's wedding! I completely forgot!"

Dovi laughed. "Obviously. But you're basically ready, no?"

Gali took a breath, calming herself. "Yeah, I laid out my dress, and my *sheitel* is done. Guess I just need jewelry and makeup. I can be ready in…thirty-five minutes. How about you?"

Dovi groaned and tilted his yarmulke over his eyes. "Do we have to go?" he asked plaintively.

Gali gave him a sympathetic smile. Her Aunt Elky was making her first wedding. Her oldest son, Michoel, had finally found his *zivug* after years of searching for the right one, and this wedding was all anyone in the family could talk about for the past few months. It was to be a "destination wedding" as neither side actually lived in Eretz Yisrael.

Gali loved weddings; people didn't bring their kids with them there. But this wedding was one she would have gladly passed up. Aunt Elky was...something else. Every single phone conversation she had with her aunt — every single one! — ended with her aunt's not-so-subtle hints as to the fact that she hoped Gali finally had some good news to share. Gali hated dashing these hopes every time they spoke, but honestly, it was really none of her aunt's business.

In any case, Gali's mother, who hadn't been able to fly in for this wedding due to work obligations, had reminded her at least five times to photograph the event minute by minute, so Gali knew she had to be there, and on time. Still, her utter reluctance to go prompted her to encourage Dovi to take a nap while she did her makeup. Then, after her face was done, she sat on her bed, flipping through a book, before working up the energy to slip on her dress. It was a silver creation, hard lace on top, a floor-length tulle skirt, and a leather, coral-colored belt. Her *sheitel* was pulled gently to the side, and her diamond studs and linked bangles finished the look. She knew she looked beautiful, but it didn't seem important just then. All she wanted was to be wearing a loose black dress, like her sister Chana would surely be sporting. Chana was expecting her sixth child. She was two years younger than Gali.

She sighed and picked up the baby lotion she had purchased earlier. She inhaled its scent, letting it fill her with excitement. This time next week, she'd be cradling a newborn baby in her arms. And when Aunt Elky called her to rehash every detail of the wedding — which Gali was sure she would do — Gali would have plenty to tell her.

But in the meantime, she really needed to wake Dovi. They had a wedding to attend.

CHAPTER TWELVE

The lobby of the David Citadel Hotel was streaming with wedding guests. Large easels were set up, directing the flow of people toward the bottom floor. Gali and Dovi entered, eyes widening at the elegant ambiance. They peered over the railing at the reception set up below.

Dovi whistled. "She really knows how to throw a party, Aunt Elky."

Gali was speechless. The smorgasbord seemed to go on for miles, burgundy tablecloths draping small round tables, each one laden with a different delicacy. There was a carving station, sushi towers, a make-your-own-smoothies booth, and ice sculptures.

"It's, um, very not Israeli," she noted aloud.

Dovi looked at her and laughed. "Um, yes."

"Ready to face the music?" Gali asked him.

Dovi bowed. "I'm ready whenever you are, m'lady." The two smiled at each other and headed toward the elevator.

"Gali!" someone shrieked the moment the elevator doors opened.

Gali looked up to see Aunt Elky's two teenage girls, Bashie and Shani, bearing down on her.

"Hi, girls! Mazel tov!" she said brightly.

The girls squealed and hugged her.

"So, Gali, what do you think of our gowns?" Shani asked, a bit anxiously.

Gali smiled inwardly. At thirteen and fifteen, the gown you wear to your brother's wedding is one of the most major decisions of your life, and it was important to validate that, Gali knew.

"Stand back. Let me take a good look at you," she ordered.

The two girls jumped backward and stood still.

Gali looked them up and down. "Gorgeous," she declared. "Absolutely stunning, both of you."

The girls threw her grateful looks.

"Come," Bashie said, taking Gali by the arm. "My mother was just asking about you. She'll want to know that you're here."

Gali swallowed hard and looked over at Dovi, who just rolled his eyes back at her in response.

The fun had officially begun.

ৡ

"Psst."

Gali spun around, startled. There was Dovi, peeking out from behind a potted plant in the empty lobby. She grinned and walked toward him as fast as her heels could take her.

"Hi," she whispered, ducking behind the plant as well. "Why are we hiding?"

Dovi took a deep breath, "Because your uncle keeps trying to drag me over to different *rabbanim* to get *brachos*. I can't handle it anymore."

Gali laughed mirthlessly. "Ah, I see. Well, did anyone give you a hug and whisper, '*Simchos* by you soon'? Or was that comment reserved only for lucky ol' me?"

The two stood there quietly, lost in their sad thoughts.

Suddenly, Dovi spoke. "Want to get out of here?" he asked, jabbing his thumb in the direction of the hotel's main doors.

Gali sighed. "You know we can't do that. Aunt Elky will know I disappeared, and I'd never hear the end of it. Besides, I told my mother I'd take pictures for her, remember?"

Dovi looked thoughtful. "Then how about we just go out for a little walk and come back in twenty minutes?"

Gali's smile was genuine for the first time that night. "I'm in."

Quickly, before any of the wedding party could spot them and stop them, they half-ran out of their hiding place and headed to the doors and outside.

"They mean well," Gali said once they were a good half block away from the hotel.

Dovi grimaced. "Yeah, but can't they 'mean well' to someone else instead, maybe?"

Gali exhaled. "I know."

The two of them walked and talked, and twenty minutes came and went. Outside, traffic roared, and wedding music played faintly in the distance, but all they heard was each other, as both Gali and Dovi basked in the comfort of being with someone who truly understood.

CHAPTER THIRTEEN

The streets whizzed by with unusual haste. Driving in Jerusalem was usually a patience-trying event, but today their car was speeding through the city with barely a taxi to cut them off.

Gali looked at Dovi and wondered if he felt as nervous as she did. He looked relaxed, his shirt sleeves rolled up and his yarmulke tilted at a jaunty angle on his head, as he sang along with the CD that was playing softly in the rented car. But looks could be deceiving, she knew. After all, she probably didn't look nervous to the point of nausea, but that was exactly how she felt.

She swiveled in her seat to check on the baby paraphernalia that filled up the back. Car seat, check. Blanket, check. Pacifier, window shade, baby bottle, check, check, check.

She turned back around to find Dovi smiling at her. "What?" she asked defensively.

"You know that was the third time you checked everything, right?"

Gali blushed. "I just...don't want to forget anything."

His smile relaxed, almost sadly. "I know, Gal. I know."

They pulled up in front of a building on the outskirts of Ezras Torah. "This is it," Dovi announced.

Gali's hands were shaking; it took her three tries to unbuckle her seat belt. Dovi went to the back to take out the infant seat, while she gathered up the blanket and the pacifier.

"Gali."

She turned to look at him. He cleared his throat and rubbed his nose.

"We can walk away now, you know. There is no legally binding contract or anything that says we have to do this. Just say the word, and we can head back into the car and drive off to Green's, drink some overpriced coffee, and then go back home. Because Gali, I can't stand to watch you get hurt. And I'm scared that's all this will lead to." He took a deep breath and braced himself for her reaction.

She stared at him, and then her features hardened into a mask of determination. "This is what I want, Dovi. I want a baby. Even if it means I'll have to let him go eventually. If I can have even one night without my arms and heart being achingly empty, then I would do it. But here I'm getting the chance to have *months* tasting the joys of motherhood! How can I not grab this opportunity? What if it's my only chance, Dovi?" Dovi looked at her, but said nothing.

She wiped the tears she hadn't even noticed had begun to fall and straightened her shoulders. "So come. Let's go meet our baby!"

Chaviva's oldest sister, Bracha Grossberg, was warm and bubbly and looked like a very young version of everybody's favorite *bubby*. She was the one in charge of her sister Shoshana's care.

"Come in, come in," she said with a smile, ushering Dovi and Gali into a small kitchen that smelled of fresh chocolate chip cookies.

They chatted about trivialities while Bracha poured them drinks. Gali clutched her glass with both hands to get them to stop shaking.

Then Bracha cleared her throat. "I guess we should get right down to it... Shoshana is still very unwell. It could be months before she is ready to embrace her responsibilities as a mother, and even longer before she is ready to take care of her new baby. After her last birth, she was unable to resume parenting for a solid half a year, maybe even a little more. So we are estimating an eight-month stay with you. If anything changes, we will give you a month's notice; we understand you have lives and cannot be subjected to sudden turns of events." She gazed at Gali, and Gali saw compassion and kindness in her green eyes.

Gali's heart warmed. "So...when can I see the baby?" she asked hesitantly.

Bracha smiled widely. "Right now!" She turned to the kitchen doorway. "Malkie!" she called. "Can you bring Yair here?" Gali's heart raced, and her cheeks felt unusually hot.

A girl of perhaps fifteen made her way slowly into the kitchen, cradling a small bundle wrapped in a yellow receiving blanket. She walked toward her mother uncertainly, but Bracha shook her head. "No, no, give him to her," she said softly, gesturing to Gali.

Gali held out her arms, taking no notice of the tears sliding out from under her lashes. Malkie placed him gently into her grasp.

"This is Yair," Bracha said. "Yair Weiss."

The baby was warm and soft and so very real. Gali gasped as he opened his small eyes and seemed to look right at her. Then he yawned, closed his eyes again, and promptly fell asleep. Gali laughed aloud and looked up to see Bracha and Dovi both blinking away tears.

"I'm confident Yair will be in good hands," Bracha said quietly.

More was said, wishes for *hatzlachah* were conveyed, and numbers were exchanged, but all Gali took out of that meeting was a small, trusting baby and a new lease on life.

⇨

GALI FELL INTO THE ROLE OF MOTHERHOOD with glee, grace, and gratitude.

"Look, Dovi!" she called happily when, a few days later, he walked in from second *seder*. "I have spit-up on my shirt!"

Dovi laughed at her excitement. "Whoo-hoo!" he cheered, grateful for the light that was shining from her eyes. "Where's Yair?"

"Sleeping," she said, while filling up a laundry basket with all of the baby's stained clothing. "How was your day?" she asked tentatively. These days she was always unsure of how that simple question would be received by him.

Dovi sighed. "Great," he said. "Just great."

Gali turned to look at him. "Just because you're not the only man in this house anymore doesn't mean I can't still see right through you," she teased gently.

Dovi smiled. "Oh, I know you can, don't worry," he said, shrugging off his coat. "Let me just go and say hello to the baby, and then I'm ready to eat. It smells yum!"

Gali smiled. She'd made spaghetti and meatballs, Dovi's favorite, in between feeding, changing, soothing, and just watching Yair.

Dovi's phone, which had fallen from his pocket onto the couch when he'd taken off his coat, rang. Still lost in daydreams in which little Yair played center stage, Gali almost didn't glance at the screen. But she did, and the name *Avrami Meyers* flashed before her eyes.

Immediately, she felt herself coming down hard from her fluffy clouds of happiness. She did not like that man. Not one little bit.

"Avrami Meyers called," Gali said conversationally at supper as Dovi took a big forkful of spaghetti.

He nearly choked, and strands of spaghetti came flying out of his mouth, landing on the table in front of him. "He did? You answered?" he asked, not meeting his wife's eyes.

"He did," she confirmed. "And I didn't. But your cooking class is over, isn't it? I didn't know you were still keeping in touch with him."

Dovi was silent for a moment, playing with his cup. When he spoke, he still refused to meet her gaze. "Yes, I'm keeping up with him. The truth? We're friends, we really are. I didn't tell you because I know you don't like him, but frankly, I do! He's not judgmental, and he gets what I'm going through..."

Gali looked at him. "Does he? Because I don't think *you* even get what you're going through, Dovi."

The baby started to cry then, a sad, plaintive wail.

Gali leaped to her feet. "I sure don't," she said sadly, and walked out to soothe Yair, while Dovi gazed morosely after her.

CHAPTER FOURTEEN

Winter usually blanketed the city in a layer of wet chill. Gali had never liked the cold, and even in Yerushalayim, where winters were generally mild, she'd become accustomed to feeling a little down by the time January rolled around. But this year, things were different. This year, she had a baby, and that made everything somehow brighter, warmer.

"I'm taking Yair for a walk," she told Dovi after lunch one day.

Dovi raised his eyebrows. "Sounds nice..." he said cautiously. "Where are you guys going?"

Gali swallowed. "The park," she whispered, blushing.

The buildings on the block all opened into a park in the back, a sort of shared backyard. It was the perfect set-up for young families: mothers could send the older ones out with the younger ones, while keeping a careful watch on everyone from their balcony or window. Yelled conversations were a frequent thing as mothers called children inside for dinner and kids called to their parents if anyone got hurt or needed a drink.

It was a beautiful arrangement — and Gali hated it. She avoided it like the plague. More than that, she pretended it didn't exist. She pretended she didn't see girls younger than her juggling families of four or five children; pretended she didn't notice the newly married girls ten years her junior proudly pushing brand-new carriages across the pavement; and most of all, she pretended she didn't hear the little girls and boys calling out "Mommy, Mommy!" all afternoon long, like little stings into an already open wound.

"Gali?"

She blinked, startled out of her reverie by her husband's voice. "Sorry, what was that you said?"

Dovi arched an eyebrow. "I was just asking if you honestly think it's a good idea to go to the park. I'm not so sure about this..."

She laughed. "Wow, this conversation would sound ridiculous to an outsider." She grew serious. "But I think I really want to go. I mean, this is my chance, right?"

"I guess so," Dovi said doubtfully. "Good luck, Gals. I'm rooting for you."

She smiled at him and went off to find the adorable teddy bear snow suit she'd bought for Yair.

೭✢

SHE SPENT ALMOST AS MUCH TIME getting dressed as she had before her first date. After ensuring that she looked right, she picked up the baby. Gali still got the chills every time she held him. He was just so small and warm, and he looked at her with such trusting eyes. She smiled at him and stroked his soft cheek before bundling him into the snow suit and fitting a matching hat over his downy head. She secured him into the designer bassinet carriage she'd borrowed from Dovi's cousin. It was a bit loud for her taste, but he did look adorable in it. One last look in the mirror, and they were off.

She took the elevator all the way down to the bottom floor, to the door that opened into the park. She hesitated one more minute, and then, squaring her shoulders, she pushed the carriage out.

She blinked in the bright sunlight and took a moment to survey the area. The benches by the swings were filled with the older crowd, the mothers with daughters old enough to obsess over whose turn it was for the swings. By the slides were the mothers of toddlers, watching their kids stubbornly sit on the bottom of the tunnel slides while the older kids hollered at them to move, and over by the water fountains were the mothers of infants, standing and talking while rocking their carriages back and forth.

All right then, water fountain it was. She walked over with practiced nonchalance and settled herself onto a bench. A second later, the seat next to her was occupied.

"Gali Rothman, in the park! I can*not* believe it!"

Gali smiled at her neighbor. "Believe it, Elisheva. I'm right here."

Elisheva leaned over the carriage. "So this is the little cutie, huh? Wow, he's gorgeous. Does his mother also have green eyes?"

Gali shrugged. "Well, I never met his mother, but I know both his aunts do."

Elisheva cooed over Yair a little longer, and then she pulled Gali off the bench. "Come meet the gang," she said, leading Gali over to the group of young mothers.

After introductions were made, the conversation turned to recipes. "I'm telling you, I have never made a good pot of chicken soup. It's either too much salt, or too bland," a pretty redhead complained.

Gali cleared her throat. "I have a foolproof recipe for chicken soup," she offered.

"You do?" the girl gasped. "Can I have it, like, now, please? I'm having seven *bachurim* over on Friday night, and I can't mess it up again..."

Gali felt the weight in her stomach disappear. She was in! She was one of the crowd, just another young mother in the park, exchanging recipes and baby tips on a sunny winter's day. She was laughing more animatedly than she had in years, nodding along as the redhead, whose name was Bashie, explained how she had turned her white tablecloth blue, when they were joined by another young mother Gali didn't know.

"Hi, Esti," Elisheva greeted her.

Esti waved cheerfully at them all, bouncing her little pink bundle up and down. "Hey, everybody! Oh my goodness, I thought I'd never get out; she was in such a bad mood! But *baruch Hashem*, here we are! Wait, who's this?" she asked, smiling at Gali.

Elisheva made the introductions. "Gali, meet Esti Brander. Esti, meet Gali Rothman."

Gali smiled, but Esti did not. Her eyes widened, and her lips parted into an O. "*Gali Rothman?!* Omigosh, like, Avigail bas Esther?" She gasped. "We have a Tehillim group for you every Friday night! I can't believe we didn't know you had a baby! Mazel tov, *baruch Hashem*, I cannot believe this! Wait till I tell the group!"

Gali stared at the girl as she rambled on. This wasn't happening. This couldn't be happening. She felt her eyes smart. No, she would not cry; she refused. She gulped. "I have to go," she said, and then she made a beeline toward the building door. As if on cue, Yair opened his tiny mouth and began to scream.

She burst into her apartment just as the tears worked their way loose. She steered the stroller into the living room, blinded by the rivers streaming from her eyes, and banged right into Dovi.

"Hey," he said. "Hey! What happened? Gali! Are you okay? Gali?"

She couldn't tell him about it right then; it was all too much.

"You were right," she managed to choke out. "Can you take care of Yair? I have to...I need to..." And without specifying exactly what it was that she needed, she fled toward the bedroom, leaving behind a bewildered Dovi and a still-crying baby.

CHAPTER FIFTEEN

The appeal of pushing a wagon with an infant seat was still going strong. Gali took items off of the shelf with a permanently goofy smile on her face. She paused every now and then to coo at Yair, taking pleasure in how his beautiful green eyes crinkled at her in what she was sure was a smile.

The events of that afternoon in the park still rankled, but she had, for the most part, gotten over it. She had overreacted, she knew, and she felt she'd disappointed herself. "I usually act with much more poise than that," she'd said regretfully to Dovi.

He had laughed. "Gal, you are the most poised person I have ever met. You're also human, though."

He had found the whole thing unbelievable. When Gali had finally calmed down enough to tell him what had happened, a look of anger had surged across his normally calm face. The anger was soon replaced, though, with a loud, room-shaking guffaw.

"Of all the people in the neighborhood you could have met on your first outing at the park, you had to meet a person with this kind of tact — or, should I say, lack thereof!"

Gali's lips had twitched as she began to see the funny side of the incident, too. And soon they were both laughing, their peals of mirth waking the baby, who had glanced around as if to ask whether or not his caretakers had gone crazy. And that was that.

Now Gali shook her head, turned into the paper goods aisle — and then stopped.

You have got to be kidding, she thought, exasperated. For there, deliberating over the colored napkins, was Esti Brander herself.

ॐ

It was day one of seminary, and they were taking their first trip to the Kosel. Gali smoothed her blouse down, tied her thick hair back with a scrunchie, and grabbed a water bottle.

"You coming?" she called to her roommate. She would've added her name, but she couldn't for the life of her remember what it was. The redhead was Tova, that she remembered, and the tall, thin blond was... Gali glanced around for a clue. There, a siddur. She reached out and picked it up. "Fraidel Raiza" was embossed in gold on the front.

Right, Fraidy! Gali put the siddur back down, and a piece of paper fluttered out. She bent down to pick it up, but Fraidy got there first.

"I have it," she said quietly.

Gali stepped back, uncertain. Had she intruded on her roommate's privacy? "I'm sorry... I-I just..." she stammered, her usual cool ruffled.

Fraidy's eyes were shuttered, her shoulders hunched, but then she sighed and her features relaxed. "It's okay," she said. "It's just my sister's name. I guess if we're going to be roommates, I should tell you both now." Her words stretched to include Tova, too. "My sister Shainee has been married six years. She still doesn't have children." She waited for the sympathetic "oy's" and sighs to pass before continuing. "Maybe you both can daven for her today. Shaina Leah bas Henya."

They'd davened for Shainee that day, and every day after that. In the spring, the three of them went to the Kosel for forty days to daven for her. And the following year, Shainee gave birth to healthy twin boys...

ॐ

THE GROCERY WAS TEEMING with its usual Erev Shabbos crowds. Couples walked through the aisles together, debating the merits of different brands and prices. Exhausted mothers pushed overflowing wagons, their feet shuffling along as they perused scribbled lists. Children ran around, getting in people's way and knocking things over. Gali stood in middle of it all, completely oblivious to the commotion around her. Her gaze was fixated on the shiny blond *sheitel* of Esti Brander...or was it the blond hair of her old roommate Fraidy?

Esti couldn't possibly have any idea as to the amount of pain she had caused Gali that day. Never before had Gali been referred to by her "Tehillim name." It hadn't just been humiliating; it was more than that. The comment, as well-intentioned as it had been, had knocked down the carefully constructed tower of self-confidence that Gali had erected. It had robbed her of her pride and grace and had left her cold, bared, and raw in front of everyone.

But still, it *had* been well-intentioned. Shaking her head, Gali threw her shoulders back determinedly and marched her wagon over to Esti. She tapped her on the shoulder.

Esti spun around, startled. Her eyes widened when she saw Gali. "Aviga— I mean, Gali, hi!" Then, as if remembering how Gali had run off on her before, she fell silent, her pale cheeks flushing red.

Gali felt bad for the girl, and she felt bad that she was the cause of her discomfort. "Esti, please don't be embarrassed. I just wanted to say thank you. Thank you for *davening* for me. I'm sure it's helping me, somehow, somewhere... I can use all the *tefillos* I can get."

Whatever Esti had thought Gali was going to say, this was not it. "Oh!" she stuttered, shocked. "I, we, um, you're welcome!"

"Okay, thanks again..." Gali smiled at her. "I'm happy we met each other. Oh, and Esti?" She raised her eyes to meet Esti's, and there was a deep, entreating plea in them that could not be ignored. "Please continue *davening* for me," Gali whispered.

Then she turned on her heel, and sharing a little smile with Yair, went to pay for her groceries, the tumult around her sliding back into focus, like a camera taken off zoom.

CHAPTER SIXTEEN

The two weeks' leave the clinic had happily given her to bond with her foster baby were now up, much to their relief and Gali's dismay. She had enjoyed every single second she spent at home with Yair. The role of foster mother felt natural to her; it made her glow from the inside, and the baby flourished. But now it was time to reenter the real world.

"Just make sure his hat covers his ears," she instructed Dovi, fussing over the stroller.

Dovi suppressed a smile. "Of course, boss," he said, saluting. Gali rolled her eyes, laughing, and turned away.

"Oh, wait!" She hurried over to the baby again. "Did I pack diapers?" She reached for the diaper bag, but Dovi pulled it out of her reach. "Yes, Gali, you packed diapers. You already checked. Twice. I forbid you, for your own sake, to check again."

Gali mock-pouted, but relented. "Okay, fine! Have a great time, but just, if it gets cold, please don't stay out, alright?" She gave the baby one more kiss and hurried to catch the bus.

Settling into her seat, she marveled at the changes in her life. Here she was, with bags under her eyes, her arm sore from when Yair fell asleep on it, and a husband who was *not* on his way to first *seder*, but rather was going to spend the day in the park and overseeing naptimes. She sighed, wondering if her happiness was on a scale, so that if one side tipped too much, something else would have to crop up to even things out. She gazed out the window and thought back to simpler times, when every opportunity seemed possible, and the horizon glinted pristinely, without a cloud in sight...

❧

"So, fourth date, hmm? They say it's a big deal."

Nineteen-year-old Gali laughed, lowering her eyes so the eager ye-shivah bachur sitting across from her wouldn't see the excitement there. "Do they?" she asked, arching an eyebrow.

"They do..." the tall boy said with a smile. "So, what do you want to know?" he asked.

Gali smiled. "Who said there's something I still want to know?"

Dovi grinned and rubbed his yarmulke across his head, causing his hair to stand straight up. He looked like an overgrown bar mitzvah boy.

Gali took a sip of her Sprite and sat back in her armchair. "Okay, fine. How about...where do you see yourself in five years?" she asked slowly.

Dovi sat back as well. "Five years? She says she has no questions, and then she slams me with a biggie!"

Gali blushed. "I'm sorry, I didn't mean—"

"I'm kidding!" he said. "It's a fair question... Well, I guess I'd have to say I don't really know... I mean, right now, I really love just sitting and learning. And I guess I'm just concentrating on that."

Gali smiled. She liked his answer. It showed the deep feelings he had for his Torah learning, as well as his honesty.

But Dovi wasn't finished. He had a faraway look in his eyes as he spoke. "I guess...wherever I am in five years, I just want to be the sort of person..." — he lowered his voice, until he was practically whispering — "...that would make Hashem proud." His ears were bright red.

Gali looked at him and felt her eyes well up with tears...

ॐ

GALI BLINKED, shaking off the memories. She looked out the window and saw that the bus was approaching her stop. She felt excited; it was good to be back. Her short hiatus had given her a much-needed energy boost, and now she was ready to be there for all of her clients, even — especially — for Aviva.

She walked off the bus and sent up a silent prayer for Dovi and Yair and another short one for success in her work. Then, squaring her shoulders, she slipped on her sunglasses and started up the block toward the large building with the words "Healthways" emblazoned on it.

ॐ

SHE FELT LIKE A CONQUERING HERO returning from the battle-front. Coworkers kept coming up to her, hugging her, wishing her well, and asking about the baby. She dutifully pulled out pictures, and everyone crooned over his black spiky hair and bright green eyes. There was an awkward moment when an intern asked if he looked like her husband because he looked nothing like her, but a brief "he's my foster child" set her straight, and Gali refused to let it bring her down.

After the mini welcome-back party, she wandered into the kitchen to grab a cup of coffee. Sipping the soothing brew, she glanced at her schedule for that day.

10:30: Meet with Natalia for private counseling

11:30: Oversee interns at group therapy

Gali groaned. She hated being a mentor for the interns. She always felt too judgmental and bossy and was sure they silently agreed.

12:15: Meet with Aviva, do a weigh-in

1:15: Break

2:00: Family therapy with Mimi and her parents

She sighed. It was going to be a long, long day. She decided to call Dovi quickly before diving in.

"Hey!" he said happily.

She smiled, glad that she was still able to make him happy. "How are my men doing?" she asked, lowering her voice.

Dovi laughed. "Well, in the hour since you've gone, Yair has slept... and that's basically it."

She sighed. "I'm missing out on all the fun over there."

Dovi's voice became sympathetic. "It's hard to be back, huh?"

She made a pouty face that he couldn't see. "Yeah...and I have a long day ahead of me..."

"*Hatzlachah,*" Dovi wished her, and they hung up.

She turned around to find Rachel standing there, looking guilty. "I'm not eavesdropping," she said quickly.

Gali giggled. "If you were, then I'm sorry for the boring conversation."

Rachel blushed and laughed. "Okay, I overheard... It's hard to be away from him, huh?" she asked softly.

Gali looked at the floor, wondering how much was okay to share in the workplace. But this was Rachel, with whom Gali had been trying to form a relationship for so long. Maybe sharing her feelings like this would help eradicate some of the discomfort Rachel felt around her.

"I guess..." She stopped and then started again. "I guess I just know our time together is limited, so I'm just wondering why I'm here and not at home, holding him and kissing up his chubby cheeks... You know what I mean?"

Rachel nodded seriously. "Yes, I hear what you're saying." Then, on impulse, she smiled. "Baby cheeks are my favorite, too," she added with a wink.

The two stood together, a companionable silence that was blessedly free of uneasiness hanging between them.

Then Rachel spoke again, tentatively. "But Gali, Yair is home with your husband, right? If you're not spending time with him now, at least he's got his father. But your patients here, they've got no one... They need you. Not to be dramatic, but your help can even be the difference between life and death for them. You know that's true for some of these girls..."

Gali thought of Aviva's pinched white face and Natalia's watery eyes. "You're right, Rachel," she said, reaching out a hand and squeezing the other woman's. "Thank you for reminding me of that," she said softly.

She squared her shoulders and marched off to her first session, at peace with where she was for the moment.

CHAPTER SEVENTEEN

She pushed open the apartment door wearily, dreaming about cuddling with Yair before having to put up dinner. She stopped in the entranceway. Was that garlic bread she smelled? She followed the scent hesitantly into the kitchen, where classical music could be heard playing softly on the sound system.

Dovi stood at the counter, his back to her, slicing cherry tomatoes. She stood there for a moment, exhaustion forgotten, and she felt a huge surge of gratitude to Hashem for giving her such a wonderful husband.

He turned just then and saw her. "Hi," he said softly, waving his knife.

Gali smiled back. "You made dinner." It was more of a statement than a question, but he nodded.

"Go look in the dining room," he said with a wink.

Smiling bemusedly, Gali walked into the other room and stopped at the sight. The table was set with china, a bouquet of roses stood in a vase in the middle of the table, and Yair was sleeping peacefully in his bassinet, with a little sign taped to it. *Happy First Day Back, Mommy Gali!* it said in proud, red letters.

Gali laughed and leaned in to kiss his little nose. He sighed sleepily, and she felt her heart swell. She couldn't believe how much she had missed him.

She went back into the kitchen, where Dovi was now tossing lettuce. "Dovi, you are too much," she said gratefully. "I can't believe you did all of this!"

Dovi smiled. "Well, from your ten phone calls and five text messages, I sort of picked up on the feeling that it was hard for you to be back."

Gali laughed. "Oh, was that it? I thought I must have called at least twenty times."

"No, t'was a mere ten," Dovi said, and they both laughed. "Anyway, I figured you might need a little something to cheer you up."

Gali smiled. "Well, you were right. Yum, what are we having?" she asked, rubbing her hands together.

Dovi put on an Italian accent. "Well, first we are having garlic bread with tomato butter, then Caesar salad, and last but not least, tilapia and lasagna."

Gali's mouth dropped open. "Are you joking? That sounds incredible!"

Dovi pointed at the sink. "Go wash. I'm just dressing the salad."

After washing, the two sat in companionable silence for a few minutes, savoring the crunchy bread and tangy butter.

"I have a feeling this has around two thousand calories a bite, but

I really don't care," Gali said dreamily, spreading some more tomato butter onto her bread. "I'm serious, Dovi, this is unbelievably delicious. You can be a professional chef!"

Dovi put down his fork, a leaf of lettuce still dangling from its prongs. "Funny you should say that," he said slowly.

Gali looked at him, and her stomach started fluttering. "Say what?" she asked loudly, not really wanting him to answer.

"That I should cook professionally. I, uh, got a job offer today. To be a caterer. With Avrami Meyers." When Gali didn't say anything, he kept talking, his words falling and tripping out of his mouth. "I can't learn anymore, Gals. It doesn't mean anything to me anymore. Well, not as much as it used to. I mean, I enjoy it, but more textually than anything else. I can't keep doing what I'm doing. It's a farce; I'm a fake. I need to move on, Gals. I need to feel alive again. I want to make money, and I'm good at cooking. You said so yourself — I'm really good, no?"

His speech ended abruptly, and a thousand thoughts exploded in Gali's mind. Leave learning completely?! Quit the precious only *seder* he had left, the one with Rabbi Gordon? Be a caterer?! With *Avrami Meyers*?! But the one thought that took precedence over all other angry ones was: *Dovi is uncertain. He's waiting for me to say that I believe in him, that I know he could do it.*

And so, dredging up superhuman strength to push down everything else she wanted to tell him, all she said was, "Yes. You'd make an incredible caterer. This is the best food I've ever tasted."

Dovi's grateful smile almost filled the large hole that had just opened up in her heart. But she ignored this as she continued to eat food that had suddenly lost all its flavor.

WHEN REBBETZIN GORDON answered the door for her, she didn't ask any questions.

"Is...is the Rav available now?" Gali stammered, feeling foolish for not having called ahead first.

"He's just on a phone call," Rebbetzin Gordon said kindly, "but he should be done soon. I'll tell him you're here." She led Gali into the dining room and pulled out a chair for her. Gali sank into it, feeling detached from her surroundings.

The Rebbetzin turned to go.

"Please," Gali said suddenly. "Can you...can you stay with us, too?"

"Of course." The older woman gave her a reassuring smile. "Let me just go and get us some hot drinks. I'll be right back."

Gali nodded and tried to return the smile, but her face felt tired and old. She looked around the room, at the pictures and paintings of *gedolim* interspersed with family portraits of children and grandchildren, and all she felt was a deep-rooted sense of despair. She would never have either of those things in her home, it seemed, not the children and not the *gedolei Torah*. She would just have bare, empty walls...

"Gali?"

She blinked, and there was Rebbetzin Gordon, balancing three mugs of tea and a plate of cookies on a tray.

"Gali, the Rav is off the phone now. Should I ask him to come in?" Rebbetzin Gordon asked, her brow crinkled.

Gali nodded. "Yes, please," she said hoarsely.

Soon the three of them were seated around the dining room table.

The Rebbetzin has style, Gali thought absently, eyeing the flowered table-runner.

Rabbi Gordon cleared his throat. "Mrs. Rothman, I'm sure Dovi told you that I went to see him the other day."

Gali nodded, and after making a *brachah*, she took a sip of tea. It was hot and sweet and it filled her insides, giving her strength. "He told me," she said. "He also told me that he...pushed the Rav away."

Rabbi Gordon chuckled. "Don't worry about that. The relationship between a *rebbi* and a *talmid* is very different than the relationship between a husband and a wife, of course, and I know that with Dovi, his pushing me away is just a temporary thing. But Mrs. Rothman, what I want to know is how *you* are faring with all of this."

Gali looked at Rebbetzin Gordon, silently supporting her husband, and she lost any vestiges of calm she'd had. "I'm not! Not at all!" she cried. "Faring, that is. I'm not faring, I'm not okay, and I'm so lost. My husband, my rock, my best friend, is turning into a stranger before my very eyes and" — here she buried her face in her hands — "it's all my fault."

Her tears splashed onto the wooden table. "If we could only have a baby, he wouldn't be like this. He wouldn't be broken. I broke him," she sobbed. "I broke him."

They let her cry for a while, and then Rabbi Gordon spoke. "Mrs. Rothman, I'm so sorry for your pain. The *Ribono Shel Olam* works in mysterious ways, and sometimes those ways leave us feeling real agony. But one thing I can tell you is that Dovi is *not* broken. I know your husband, Mrs. Rothman. He's floundering, yes; angry, sure; and he needs time and space — and, of course, your support — to get back to himself, but he's so very far from broken.

"And," Rabbi Gordon raised his voice a notch, "even if he was, it would not be your fault at all. We are just small pieces in Hashem's grand plan, and we cannot take credit for the way things turn out. All we have to do is the best we can do, and the results...those are up to Hashem."

Gali sighed, embarrassed at her outburst. She knew Rabbi Gordon was right. But still... "So what do I do now?" she whispered. "He wants to drop everything and become a caterer. A caterer!" She looked at the Rav and Rebbetzin in desperation.

"Support him," Rabbi Gordon said simply. "Being a caterer is not a bad thing. Of course it's nothing like spending your day in the *koslei beis midrash*, but for where Dovi is right now, the catering experience could be a very positive outlet. He'll feel good about himself, about the food he is preparing, about what he is creating.

"And while you support him," Rabbi Gordon continued, "let him know that you don't believe this *tekufah* is forever. Let him know you still have a lot of hope for his *ruchniyus*, that you are still fighting for him, for your old life, for a Torah life. But at the same time, give him the unconditional love and acceptance he is craving. I know this sounds impossible, but it's not, and I believe, Mrs. Rothman, that you have the inner mettle to do this."

Gali listened silently, absorbing what the Rav was saying. With a sinking feeling she realized that if she'd thought her *nisayon* was hard before, things were escalating now to a possible breaking point. She just hoped she was strong enough to withstand it all.

CHAPTER EIGHTEEN

She tucked the phone more securely under her neck and held up a cream-colored sweater. No, not professional enough. She tuned back in to the conversation.

"...And I'm thinking of setting him up with Shevy Kruger."

Gali blinked. Apparently, now they were discussing *shidduchim*. A moment ago, the topic had been Pesach plans.

"Sounds like a great idea, Ma," she murmured, reaching for a belted navy dress. Perfect. She'd wear it with a pair of flat brown boots and a big gold necklace; it would look professional, but friendly. She picked up a mustard yellow pullover and mentally matched it with a gray flared skirt.

"Gali, are you listening? I asked if you're sure you don't just want to leave Yair with Chana. Wouldn't that be easier than having Dovi stay home all day with him?"

Gali snapped to attention. "Sorry, Ma, I was just spacing out there," she apologized. "We thought about sending Yair to Chana, but we really like the idea of him sleeping in his own crib and being on his own schedule... Poor baby has been passed around enough in his short life."

Both women sighed in unison.

"Anyway," Gali continued, "it's only four days. And Dovi is crazy about the baby, so he really doesn't mind watching him the whole time. I think it'll be okay."

She spoke cheerfully, but her thoughts were far from happy. A four-day conference away from her husband and baby was perhaps the last thing she wanted to do right now. As it was, things were so unstable in her life. And here she'd just gotten back into the swing of things at work...

She imagined, just for an instant, plopping down on her bed amid her packing and spilling out her heart to her mother. But Esther Lerner was a worrier. And Gali really had no desire to add to her mother's list of daily anxieties. Her childlessness already broke her mother's heart anew each day. If she were to know that her beloved son-in-law had lost his way, Gali didn't know what her mother would do, but she didn't want to find out.

Yair woke up just then with a small whimper that melted her insides. She promised to call her mother back and went to lift the baby out of his bassinet.

"Hi, my tiny boy," she whispered, nuzzling her face in the soft downy hairs on his head. She breathed in his scent, allowing it to fill all the cracks in her heart, even if just for a minute. He blinked up at her in acknowledgment, and she felt the sadness begin to creep back into her weary being. She only had a few months left to be Yair's mother, and after that...there would be nothing. Just a long, endless stretch of empty days and lonely nights.

She could barely remember what it was like before Yair entered her life; the memories were gray and shapeless. She couldn't recall what she used to fill her life with, though she supposed her marriage used to be a lot more fulfilling. The pang that accompanied any thoughts about Dovi hit her hard, but she drove it away by tickling the baby's belly and listening to him giggle. Surely there was no sweeter sound in the entire world. She tickled him again and laughed out loud along with him. It was easier than crying.

مو

SHE PULLED THE CURTAIN BACK and stared out the window at the Tel Aviv skyline, wishing she were on her little porch back at home instead, holding Yair and watching the sun set amidst the Jerusalem hills. But the annual Jewish Social Workers' Conference was always held in the Tel Aviv Sheraton, and so, like it or not, she was here for the next few days. She sighed, and then went to get ready for the first meeting.

"Shalom, I am Talia Goldblatt," the conference coordinator said cheerfully to the room of social workers. She was a middle-aged woman wearing a bright kerchief around her head and a large smile. Gali liked her instantly and she relaxed slightly. She usually enjoyed these meetings, but now she was busy pining for Yair. She shook her head and forced herself to focus on the present.

"We'll go around in a circle, and everyone will introduce themselves," Talia said. She sat down and motioned for the woman on her right to begin.

Gali felt herself get drawn into the mood, and when it was her turn, she was more than happy to stand up and introduce herself. "Hi, my name is Gali Rothman," she said, smiling. "I'm a social worker in Healthways Eating Disorders Clinic in Jerusalem, and I love it."

She sat back down as everyone smiled back, and the next person stood up. "Hi, I'm Adele Plotnick. I'm a social worker in Brooklyn, New York. Actually, this conference just happened to coincide with my vacation, and I decided to join. I'm really looking forward to the next four days!"

Gali felt herself relax even more. On some level, she was also looking forward to the next few days. She loved what she did, and it was nice to feel like a professional again, instead of always playing the role of martyred wife, which she'd been doing so much lately. Hmm, maybe she could pick up some tips from this conference on how to deal with Dovi... She smiled inwardly. She knew Dovi would see right through any social worker persona she'd try to pull on him.

"We will be hearing now from Professor Ben Newman of London, on the topic of accessing our own conscious and unconscious biases and prejudices," Talia was saying.

Gali leaned forward; this sounded interesting. She only thought about Dovi and the baby long enough to wonder how they were doing before the lecture pulled her in.

ஐ

SHE FLOPPED ONTO THE BED and was calling Dovi before she even kicked off her shoes.

"Hello, Madame Social Worker!" Dovi's warm and friendly

voice filled the line, and Gali was suddenly overwhelmed with homesickness.

"Hello," she said morosely.

Dovi laughed. "Oh, c'mon, it's only been one day... *Nu*, so how's it going? Learned anything new yet?"

"Tons," Gali said. "They try to cram a year's worth of information into four days. But enough about me! How's my little chicken nugget?"

"Well," Dovi said, "if you mean the baby, he's doing amazingly. He's eating, sleeping, and spitting up, so pretty much business as usual."

Gali laughed, picturing Yair's tiny, cherubic face. "Yum, tell me more about him," she moaned, and now Dovi laughed.

"Well, he just blinked and yawned. I can't believe you missed it!" His voice was teasing, and Gali smiled. It was good to hear Dovi sound happy, even if she was miles away. She hoped that wasn't the reason for it... She rolled her eyes at this childish display of self-doubt.

"And how are you doing?" she asked him, more hesitantly.

"I'm great!" Dovi said brightly.

Gali closed her eyes. For twelve years, every single time she'd asked Dovi how he was or how he felt, the answer had always been "*Baruch Hashem*, great!" or "Not so good, *baruch Hashem*." Maybe she was reading too much into things, but she still felt a rush of sadness at the way Dovi had just responded to her question.

"That's good," she said softly. "Any new orders?" Dovi's catering business was really taking off, slowly but surely. Gali was doing her best to be as supportive as possible while still maintaining her standards, as per Rabbi Gordon's instructions, but it was a tight rope to walk.

"Yes!" Dovi said excitedly. "We have a yeshivah dinner next week, and a bar mitzvah the following Shabbos — someone Avrami has connections to. They could have used any caterer, you know, but they specifically wanted us for it. You got any good ideas we can do?"

Gali felt her stomach turn. She *really* didn't like Avrami Meyers. But Dovi loved his work, so she kept her mouth shut. "Hmm. Well, people are crazy over that fruity lettuce salad that you make, you know, the one with the pomegranate seeds and mandarin oranges... It's such an eye-catching appetizer. And maybe for the next course..."

They spent the next hour and a half hashing out ideas, sketching out the future events, and talking about pretty much everything, except for the obvious fact that Dovi was slowly drifting away from all that Gali held dear. When she finally bid him goodnight, it was with a wistful smile on her lips and a prayer in her heart.

అ

"WELCOME TO THE OPEN FLOOR," Talia said grandly, gesturing to the three chairs lined up in front of her. Gali yawned. She'd really stayed up too late talking to Dovi. But there was no time for personal thoughts right now. Talia was describing an activity that they would be doing.

"Three of you will have a chance to come up here and describe your most difficult case, obviously within your ability to share it. The rest of us can offer feedback and perspective on the resistance shown by the client, what might be behind it, and how the therapist might try to approach it in this situation."

Gali turned to a fresh page in her notebook, her interest piqued. Talia pointed to three different social workers, and they went forward to occupy the front chairs.

The first person stood up. It was Adele Plotnick from New York. "Hi, everybody," she said, and everyone murmured a greeting back.

"Okay, I have this one client, X. She's a typical adolescent, insecure, self-involved, and so on. The only difference between her and her peers is her father. He's her hero and role model, except when he drinks. Then he becomes her worst enemy and nightmare, all at once. She comes to me at the instruction of her school and sits there, pouting, not saying a word. I'd appreciate advice on how to handle this case."

She sat back down, and the comments started pouring forth. Some participants felt Adele should openly challenge the resistance, while others thought she should "trust the process" and sit silently, waiting until the client was ready to cooperate, however long that might take. Gali sat back, thinking about the case. A heated debate broke out, with Talia calmly mediating. Gali started to get antsy; she wanted to go call Dovi and find out how Yair had fared through the night without her. She slipped out of the room and called home.

"Gali?" Dovi sounded far away.

"Hi," she said happily. "How are you?"

"Going slightly insane," he said tiredly. "We miss you here. Yair woke up around six times last night, and every time he saw it was me and not you, he started crying."

"Aww..." Gali sighed. "He misses me! That's so cute!"

Dovi groaned. "Adorable. But don't worry about us. You just have fun there, okay?"

"Okay," Gali said, and she hung up.

For the rest of the day, all she could think about was sweet little Yair and how much she wanted to hold him.

Chapter Nineteen

He'd just hung up the phone with Gali, and already he wanted to call her back to kvetch some more about Yair's sleeping habits. But if he complained too much, he knew, she'd just run and call her sister, and Chana would rush over to take Yair, and Dovi would be left alone and aimless for the next two days. Well, not aimless — he had plenty of work for the catering business to keep him busy — but definitely alone...

"Nope, buddy, you're stuck with me," he said, leaning over Yair's carriage and tickling him. The baby gurgled in happy agreement, and then he spit up.

Dovi groaned. "And so the fun continues..." He went to get a diaper cloth and was just wiping up the little white puddle when the doorbell rang. He padded over to answer the door, very aware of his bare feet, gray sweatpants, and white t-shirt.

Avrami Meyers stood there in the doorway, his arms full of groceries.

"Move; these are heavy," he commanded Dovi, pushing past him to enter the apartment. He made his way toward the kitchen, a very annoyed Dovi following in his wake.

"Avrami, I told you I was babysitting. What on earth are you doing here?"

Avrami started pulling knives and cutting boards out of Gali's carefully organized cabinets and setting up bowls of water. "Where do you have a peeler?" he asked Dovi, opening drawers.

"Second drawer on your left," Dovi answered automatically. "So?" he asked, picking up the baby and holding him close. Yair hadn't been crying, but Dovi felt irritated, and holding the baby would prevent him from punching Avrami.

"What do you mean, 'So?' We just got a huge gig, a *sheva brachos* for the rich and famous. I'm talking a 20,000-shekel paycheck here!"

Dovi's jaw dropped. "Are you joking?" he asked, putting the baby in his swing and grabbing another peeler.

The two peeled a mountain of potatoes, planning the menu all the while. Then Avrami pulled out his iPod.

"Really?" Dovi asked, his nose scrunching in distaste at the crass music. "This is for high schoolers, man."

Avrami grinned. "Hey, I'm just as confused and unintelligent as any of them."

Dovi laughed. "No arguments on that one," he teased.

Avrami hit him with a whisk, Dovi lifted a spatula, and a sword fight broke out.

"Hiya!" Dovi shouted.

"Ooph!" Avrami responded, swinging hard and breaking a glass vase.

They stood there shamefacedly among the shards for a minute, weapons hanging loosely in their hands. Then they both burst out laughing, tears of mirth running down their cheeks, until the baby woke up with a cry.

ॐ

Six hours later, with trays of cooked appetizers cooling on the countertops, the two men reclined on the leather sofa, cold beers in their hands.

"Ah, the joys of bachelorhood," Avrami said blissfully. He took a swig of his beer.

Dovi shrugged. "Eh," he said.

"What do you mean, 'Eh?'" Avrami asked incredulously. "What more can you want? You've got the leather couch, some good pretzels, a cold beer, and blissful silence. No nagging, no preaching, no, 'Do this' or, 'Can you get me down that?'" He shuddered. "Ugh, it was like being in prison."

Dovi thought longingly of Gali's happy voice, her smile, the way she encouraged him and supported him, no matter what. "C'mon, man, you can't really mean that," he said softly to Avrami, staring at his friend.

Avrami put his head back and closed his eyes. "Oh, I do," he said. "I bet you would, too, if you really thought about it."

Dovi laughed. "If there is one thing I can promise you, old friend, it's that I will never agree with you on that. My wife, well...I'm nothing without her. Not all marriages are prisons, you know."

Avrami was silent.

Poor guy really has no idea what I'm talking about, Dovi thought. Without stopping to think his next words through, he asked, "What are you doing for Shabbos this week, Meyers? Wanna join us?"

Avami rolled his eyes and took another sip of his beer. "Can't," he said, suddenly sounding tired. "My girls are coming in this week from New York, and they'll be with me."

"So bring them along!" Dovi urged, though he was already regretting having invited Avrami to begin with. Gali would just be coming back from her conference, and she'd be exhausted...

But Avrami now looked interested. "Yeah, bro? You wanna have us all over? Let me ask the girls, and I'll let you know."

Dovi nodded, silently praying that the answer from Avrami's daughters would be no.

ے

"The girls would love to come," Avrami told him over the phone the next day.

Dovi's shoulders slumped. "Great," he said with forced enthusiasm. Just great. Gali was going to have his head for this...

He dipped his *sponga* stick into the bucket and moved it back and forth over the floor, trying to pick up the last bits of glass from the vase they'd broken yesterday. Yair gurgled happily in his swing, and Dovi looked over at him. "Hey, this stays just between us guys, alright, buddy?"

The baby's green eyes twinkled at him, and he took that as a yes. "I appreciate it," he said briskly. He looked at the shining spot on the floor. Might as well do a full job of it. Maybe Gali wouldn't be upset if she came home to shining floors.

Oh, who was he kidding? She'd be annoyed either way. Still, there was nothing like a little manual labor to get your mind off of your troubles... He played some Avraham Fried over the surround sound system. He was confused, but he still knew good music.

"Come, baby," he cooed to Yair. "Let's clean the house for Mommy Gali!"

An hour and a half later, every floor in the large apartment was sparkling, and Dovi was tired. Thankfully, Yair had fallen asleep, so there was time enough for a hot shower and a nap. Dovi honestly had no idea how women did it. Cooking, cleaning, child-raising... it was exhausting!

He wondered if taking care of a baby would be less strenuous if it were his own child, blood of his blood, flesh of his flesh. He leaned over the bassinet and stared at Yair's sleeping face. The delicate bone structure, pointed chin, spiky black hair...it was all endearing, but it was foreign to him. He pictured, for a moment, a different baby lying there, with perhaps his own light brown hair and Gali's big brown eyes...

He felt something prickle at his eyelids, and he turned away before the pain consumed him.

৵

"Oh, it is so good to be back!" Gali said happily, picking up Yair and covering his face in kisses.

Dovi grinned. "Well, we're so happy to have you back!" He truly was. Peace and quiet could be nice, unless you had a million voices of self-doubt in your head, driving you crazy. In that case, companionship was the only way to go.

He took the baby and placed him on the floor.

Gali sank gracefully onto the couch. "I'm looking forward to a quiet Shabbos, just the three of us..." She pulled at the lever on the side of the couch so that the footrest popped out, and leaned back, closing her eyes.

Dovi cleared his throat uncomfortably. "Um, that might be a problem," he said hesitantly.

Gali's eyes sprang open. "Why?" she asked suspiciously.

Dovi blushed, feeling like a little boy who'd just tracked mud all over the white carpet. "Because I invited Avrami and his daughters to spend Shabbos with us," he said.

Gali stared at him, her mouth open.

"He was rambling about marriage and prisons, and I...his daughters...then he —" Dovi knew he was being incoherent, but Gali's silence was unnerving. "Gali!" he said sharply. "Say something!"

She closed her mouth and then opened it again. "I see," was all she said.

Dovi bit his lip. "I'm really sorry," he said softly. "I shouldn't have invited them without asking you first..." He picked up Yair and waved his little hand. "We so sowwy, Mommy Gali!" he squeaked.

Gali giggled, and then sighed. "Fine! You win. Now let me sleep before I have to go grocery shopping!"

Dovi saluted. "Aye, aye, Cap'n!" he said, carrying the baby out of the room and dimming the lights on his way out.

Gali was asleep in seconds.

CHAPTER TWENTY

The sweet, yeasty smell of challah dough permeated the apartment. Gali adjusted her snood and wiped her forehead. Her kitchen reached unbearably hot temperatures when the oven was on.

Dovi ambled in just then and sniffed appreciatively. "Yum, Gals, it smells heavenly in here," he said, walking to the water cooler and passing her a cup of ice water.

"Thanks," she said. She mumbled her *brachah* quietly and took a long drink. She looked up to find Dovi eyeing her in amusement.

"You don't have to do that, you know." He pulled out a chair and sat down.

"Do what?" Gali asked defensively.

"Be afraid to say *brachos* in front of me," he said. He leaned back in his seat and stretched out his long legs.

Gali flushed. "I'm not…I mean…I, well, how am I supposed to know that?" she finally blurted out.

"Well, I still say them," he said, reaching for an apple from the fruit bowl. He made a resounding *Ha'eitz*, to which Gali responded with a confused amen.

"So why do you?" she asked, while she gathered the ingredients for her famous blondies. She lined them up on her marble island and reached for a mixing bowl.

"Habit, I guess," Dovi said through crunches. "I guess I'd feel… empty if I didn't."

Gali thought about it. "That makes sense," she said after a minute. "What about…Avrami Meyers?"

Dovi glanced up at her. "What about him?" he asked, his voice even.

"Does he make *brachos*?"

Dovi gave a half-smile. "No clue," he said. He gave a little chuckle. "It's not like a club, where we all do the same thing and follow the same rules for life."

Gali mixed her batter, a smile breaking out across her face. "Imagine if it were," she said, snickering.

"The Ex-Yeshivah Guys Against *Brachos* Club," Dovi supplied, snorting. They both cracked up.

"That is the least funny thing you ever said," Gali said with a sigh, wiping her eyes. "But as a social worker, I can tell you that gallows humor is very therapeutic."

Dovi gave one last laugh. "I can see that," he said. "Anyway, let me help you with something. It's my fault we're having all these guests when you're so exhausted, so put me to work."

Gali plunked the package of chicken down in front of him. "Great,

Chef Rothman, amaze me with your talents. And after the chicken, you can make the potato kugel and the brisket, okay?"

Dovi rolled up his sleeves. "You got it, boss!" he said, and they worked in companionable silence until the last ingredient was put away and the birds were sending out their first few songs to greet the morning. Only then did they fall into bed in exhausted states of accomplishment.

ﻬ

GALI PLUMPED UP THE PILLOWS on the guest beds one more time, straightened the comforters, and set down a bowl of chocolates and a bottle of water. Perfect.

She went to give Yair a bath and instructed Dovi to transfer the food onto the *blech*. She was just sponging water onto the baby's little head, singing softly, when she heard the door open and Dovi's laugh ringing around the apartment. The guests had arrived. She rolled her eyes; she really had no energy for this.

She quickly diapered and dressed the baby, brushed his soft hair, and, sending up a prayer for strength, she walked into the kitchen. Seeing that Dovi had served everyone blondies and juice, she mouthed him a thank you. He smiled.

Gali nodded cordially to Avrami and then turned to the girls. "Hello, how are you? I'm Gali," she greeted them.

"Hi, I'm Shiri," the younger one said, dimpling, and Gali's heart melted.

Gali turned to the older girl, who was perched silently on a bar stool, and smiled at her. "And what's your name?"

The girl flipped her long red hair over one shoulder. "Ora," she said, fiddling with the watch on her thin wrist. "Thank you for having us," she added with a small smile.

Gali looked at her, and the hairs on the back of her neck rose. "My pleasure," she said, trying to shake the eerie feeling that had taken hold of her. Quickly, she asked Dovi to show Avrami and his daughters to their rooms, and then she ran to shower and get dressed.

Soon she was standing in front of her candles. Yair was gurgling on his play-mat, the two sisters were deep in conversation with each other on the couch, and the men were heading out to shul. Gali swayed, hands over her face, and poured out her heart in prayer. She *davened* for her husband, that he return to the true path of Torah and mitzvos. Then she *davened* for a child of her own; she *davened* for Yair; she *davened* for his mother, that she should be well again; and she *davened* for the two hurting girls sitting on her living room couch. Lastly, she *davened* for her clients' recovery. Then she was done.

She uncovered her face and felt that special Shabbos calm descend onto her heart. "Good Shabbos," she said warmly to the girls. She scooped up Yair and sat across from them. "So, how old are you girls?" she asked, playing with the collar on Yair's stretchie.

Shiri answered. "I'm ten, and Ora's fourteen. We also have two brothers," she continued chattily. "We're probably going to stay in Israel now and move in with our father, but the boys wanted to stay in New York with our mother..." Ora shot her an angry look, as if Shiri had said too much, and the younger girl's voice trailed off.

"Well, it's more fun when it's just girls, anyway," Gali said smoothly. "So tell me, what do you like best about being in Eretz Yisrael?"

She continued with the small talk, until they decided to *daven*.

Then the girls followed her into the kitchen as she went to make salads and put out the fish.

Gali took out the stack of fish plates and began serving the salmon. "Do you two eat fish?" she asked.

Shiri scrunched her nose. "I don't like fish, and Ora doesn't eat anything," she said with a giggle.

Gali looked up sharply just in time to see Ora step on Shiri's foot. The hairs on the back of her neck were up again, and she felt a prickling sensation creeping down her spine.

"Teenagers on diets, huh?" she said to Shiri, trying for a light tone. But Shiri just shrugged sullenly. Ora, for her part, looked furious.

"Can you bring the *chummus* to the table?" Gali asked Shiri. When she had left the kitchen, Gali turned to Ora. "Must be hard to be on a diet, what with your father being this gourmet chef and all, huh?" she asked casually, picking up a pepper and a knife. She started cutting, but out of the corner of her eye, she saw Ora turn white.

"It's not a big deal," she said quietly. "Should I cut the cucumbers?"

Gali swallowed the bile that had suddenly risen in her throat. "That'd be great, thanks," she said brightly, and the two of them sliced away in silence.

Once the meal was underway, Gali made it through Kiddush and *Hamotzi*, but then she reached her limits. "Dovi, can you help me serve the fish?" she asked sweetly, motioning to the guests to sit and enjoy.

"With pleasure," he said jovially, getting to his feet and bowing comically at the guests. He was still smiling when Gali slammed the kitchen door shut behind him.

"Do you realize that Avrami's daughter has a full-blown eating disorder?" she whispered vehemently to her husband. "That girl is so thin, a good puff of wind can blow her over!"

Dovi stared at his wife in shock, the smile sliding off of his face. "Are...are you serious?" he stammered, his eyes wide.

"Completely," she said. "I checked for the obvious indications, and she's got them all." She buried her face in her hands. "If we know this is going on, Dovi, we have to do something about it! Her father clearly has no clue how to handle teenagers, and if we don't intervene" — she looked up at Dovi, her eyes glistening — "she can die."

CHAPTER TWENTY-ONE

Where are you off to?" Gali asked Dovi lazily over her morning coffee. She was barely awake, but Dovi was already halfway out the door with his wallet and phone. Gali hated his new phone. She didn't believe in Smartphones, and until recently, Dovi had agreed with her. Now he was constantly bent over the thing, and it was driving her crazy.

"We have to go pick up our chicken order for Tuesday's dinner," Dovi said, shuffling his feet.

"By 'we,' do you mean you and Avrami?" Gali asked sharply.

He nodded.

"Well, did you tell him what I told you, you know, about his daughter Ora?"

Dovi nodded again. "I did, but he just...laughed it off. He said girls love to be thin, and he's not worried."

Gali stared at him. "Not worried? Her nails are broken, her bones jut out, and her hair is split and cracked. She has anorexia nervosa at least, if not something else as well."

Dovi looked at her helplessly. "I really need to run, Gals. We'll talk about this later, 'kay?" A moment later he was gone.

Gali sat in her empty kitchen and wondered if she should have shared with Dovi the second half of her suspicion, that Ora's eating disorder had everything to do with her father, Avrami Meyers, the very same man Dovi had just run out to meet.

IT WAS THE SORT OF DAY that hinted at spring. The world was brighter, the colors more vivid; even the people themselves were kinder. Gali sat back on the bench and tilted her face toward the sun, feeling the rays warm her skin and loving it.

She opened her eyes, blinking away the sun spots, and checked her watch. Dovi was late. She sighed, glancing around while rocking Yair's carriage with her foot. He was asleep; the motion was more for her sake than for his.

She, along with most of the people living in Israel, hated appointments at the Misrad Hapnim. The wait was unbearably long, the workers were unbelievably cranky, and you didn't always leave with what you had come for in the first place. But Yair needed a visa, and they had already rescheduled the appointment twice due to Dovi's busy catering schedule. She took a deep breath and tried not to let her annoyance overtake her. She was glad that Dovi was finally doing something with his time, but she still saw pain lingering in the shadows near his eyes, so she knew that the whole catering shebang wasn't exactly making him *happy*. But he was definitely feeling productive, and that could only be a good thing. She closed her eyes again.

"Boo!"

She jumped, eyes flying open. There was Dovi, grinning like an overeager three-year-old. "Sorry, couldn't resist," he said impishly, and she laughed despite herself.

"Not nice," she said, only half-joking. She stood up quickly, before Dovi could sit down next to her and make them even later. "We need to go right now." She took Yair's stroller and began to walk.

A moment later, she looked back. Dovi was still standing there.

"Gali," he said softly.

She had the urge to just continue walking; she had a feeling she knew what he was going to say, and she silently begged him not to.

"Gali," he said again. "I don't want to go to America for Pesach."

There it was. She felt her heart beat faster and her temper rising along with it. She turned and walked back toward him, not saying a word.

He waited until she was next to him again, and then he continued. "You didn't tell your family about my...changes, did you?"

Gali raised her eyes and stared at him, at the face that she knew so well. The light brown hair. The slightly almond-shaped eyes. The straight nose, the cleft chin, the crooked smile. It was the same Dovi she had married. But then her gaze took in the blue shirt where the white one had always been, the light-colored pants, the small yarmulke, the Smartphone clipped onto his belt, and the cooking magazine that was sticking out of his pocket.

She took a step back. The man in front of her certainly didn't seem like the Dovi she had married...but he was. She knew that, and he knew that, but her family? They didn't know that.

She swallowed and fought down the barrage of helpless tears that were threatening to overtake her, right there at the train stop. "No," she whispered. "I didn't say anything to them about it."

He looked at her, and his eyes were pleading. "Please, Gali, I can't. I can't do it," he whispered, and she knew he was answering her unspoken plea that he fake it. It was only a couple of weeks, after all; how hard would it be for him to slip back into "old Dovi" gear, just to save face in front of her family? But apparently, it was out of the question for him, and suddenly, she'd had enough.

"No," she said.

Dovi blinked, surprise taking over his expression, feature by feature. She watched his mouth open slightly, and she went on.

"Twelve years, Dovi. For twelve years we've gone to the family Seder and sat there in unspeakable pain while everything centered around those with children. We listened to nieces and nephews say the *Mah Nishtanah* and watched the candy rewards and *afikoman* hunts and *Makkos* demonstrations, all the while sitting silently, our arms empty and our faces turned to stone so that no one should guess the amount of agony in our hearts. And yet, somehow, everyone always knew anyway, and so the rest of Yom Tov would be filled with pity hugs and heart-to-hearts and eggshell-walking.

"And finally, *finally*, I can go to the Seder holding a baby too. I can dress him up in cute Yom Tov outfits, excuse myself to go change him and feed him and put him to sleep. I can join in the conversations about sleepless nights and feeding schedules and all those other discussions that I was never able to take part in. And now, *now* you don't want to go. Why? Because of the very same changes that keep me up at night, that haunt my dreams, that fill my heart and soul with worry every minute of the day. Because of those changes, you want to deprive me of this opportunity? Who *are* you, anyway, Dovi? Who *are* you?"

She stopped for breath, only now realizing that hot tears were coursing down her cheeks, that Yair was howling softly, and that a group of Israeli children was gathered around them, staring at her with mouths hanging open. She wiped her face angrily, grabbed Yair's carriage, and without looking at Dovi, she stepped onto the train that had just pulled up.

إ

SHE GOT OFF AT THE NEXT STOP. She couldn't go to the Misrad Hapnim without Dovi, especially if he didn't want her to get Yair a visa at all. That just wasn't who she was.

She ducked into a nearby store and went to the ladies' room to check her appearance. She pulled off her sunglasses. *Great,* she thought to herself with a frown. Her face was a black, smudgy mess. She washed her face, touched up her makeup with some concealer from her purse, adjusted the bangs on her *sheitel*, and straightened her shoulders. There, perfect. She leaned over Yair's carriage and gave him a pacifier to suck. Now they were both calmer.

She grabbed a pair of men's socks from a nearby rack and went to pay for them. It was the least she could do after using the store's mirror and sink. Bag in hand, sunglasses securely on, she headed back outside, her destination suddenly clear.

She was going to the Kosel. She hadn't taken Yair there yet, and now the time had come.

CHAPTER TWENTY-TWO

ovi kicked a rock angrily. It just rolled to the side, and now his foot hurt. Great, just great.

His phone beeped, and he pulled it out of his pocket automatically. He detested the thing, but it did make work so much easier.

Touching the screen, he read the text message: *Vegetable sale in market. Meet me there ASAP.* He sighed. Avrami was always finding bargains and deals for their business. Sometimes they were legitimate; other times they were...less so. Dovi shuddered at the memory of Avrami's last "deal." Two Arab workers had promised to sneak a few cartons of lettuce off their delivery truck. Dovi had put his foot down at that one, and Avrami had reluctantly agreed.

He waited for the approaching train and got on, his face flushed with regret. Gali didn't deserve what he was giving her. She was, without a doubt, the most selfless person he knew. She was kind and generous and uncomplaining. He'd watched her these past twelve years, watched as she'd accepted her lot with equanimity, never allowing her inner pain to bring her down or affect those surrounding her. He'd seen her relationship with Hashem grow stronger and stronger as she confided in Him at least a dozen times a day. She recited Tehillim daily, she *davened* both Shacharis and Minchah, and occasionally Ma'ariv, too, and she loved to find *hashgachah pratis* in her daily routine.

But seeing his wife's righteousness, in contrast to the lot she'd been given, had begun to eat away at him. He'd watch her, this burst of sunshine in the clouds that were their life circumstances, and waited to see the justice of it all. He waited for their salvation, for the end to appear in sight...but instead he was greeted with another day of watching the world go by without them. He was sick of it; he couldn't handle the pain anymore. For himself, it might have been alright. But for her? He couldn't. It messed with his head, with his faith, with everything he believed in.

Now, though, he was the one causing her pain, and he hated himself for it.

He stepped off the train and walked up the block toward the market, keeping his eyes lowered to the ground. Even with all of his anger, there were some things he wouldn't allow into his soul, and the low moral standards of this part of town was one of them.

He looked up only when he heard his name being called. There was Avrami, standing outside the market, a smirk on his face.

"Dovi, what's a yeshivah guy like you doing in this neck of the woods?" he asked mockingly, slapping Dovi on the shoulder.

Dovi gave a half-grin. "You tell me," he said.

Avrami ran his fingers through his hair. "There's an investor in there, eating breakfast at the pancake stand," he said, pointing into the belly of the market. "My cousin told him about us, and he agreed to meet. If he likes us...he might invest in a restaurant...for us!"

Dovi gaped at him. "A restaurant? I thought you said a vegetable sale. That's unreal!" He felt his pulse race, the opportunity creating castles in his mind. "Wow, he's in there right now?" he asked nervously. He smoothed his shirt down and wiped the sweat off his brow.

Avrami laughed. "Yeah, I only said that about the vegetable sale because it was too much to explain in a text. And don't worry; he's going to love you. Just one thing..." Dovi looked at him, eyes widening in ever-growing horror as Avrami plucked the yarmulke off Dovi's head and slipped it into his shirt pocket. "Lose the yarmulke, yeshivah boy," he said to Dovi, winking.

Dovi stared at him, his eyes growing hard, nausea rising up through his stomach to the back of his throat. "Are you...joking?" he finally asked, his voice shaking.

The smile slid from Avrami's face, and his eyes narrowed. "Dovi, this guy is a wealthy business tycoon from Tel Aviv. He will meet with us only once. He's in a good mood, because the pancake stand makes the best breakfast in all of Israel. We are two nobodies, with nothing to offer except for our culinary talents. Please don't blow this for both of us by refusing to take off something you don't care about anyway, okay?"

Dovi stared at his friend, at Avrami's own bare head, and the way the sun seemed to project right onto the round spot where his yarmulke had once been. Then he grabbed his yarmulke back from Avrami, spun on his heel, and ran, as fast as he could, away from the market, away from Avrami, and away from the streets that were slowly eating away at the purity of his soul.

He needed to go somewhere good; he needed to be near Gali to bask in her goodness, in her righteousness. He tried to call her, but she wasn't answering her phone.

Then an idea popped into his head: the Kosel. What holier place than that existed? He would go to the Kosel.

ও

HE ENTERED THE PLAZA AND STOPPED, staring at the Wall. The sun had turned the stones into a blinding vision, and he raised his hand to shield his eyes. He waited to feel something, anything that told him Hashem wanted him to be there, but all he felt was relief. For now, that would have to be enough.

He entered the men's section, grateful for the variety of people, for the vast differences in everyone's dress, relieved that this was one place where he wouldn't stick out like a sore thumb. He went to put his hands on the age-old stones, and he felt the tears begin to form at the corners of his eyes. It wasn't spirituality that caused him to break down; it was the knowledge that millions of people before him had cried in this very spot, and not all of them had seen salvation in their lifetimes. Would he be one of those, doomed to cry and cry for the rest of his life? Of course he knew his suffering would be repaid handsomely in *Olam Haba*...but what about in This World? Would there be a happy ending written out for him and Gali in This World, too?

He felt the request rise up from his very being, and he begged Hashem to help him figure out his life. Then he cried for a child for himself and Gali, a child of their own, and he thought about Yair, his sweet baby boy who wasn't really his, and he *davened* for him, too. Then he stepped back, drained, and began to walk backward, away from the Wall.

He reentered the courtyard and began the slow trek to the Old City, his shoulders slumped, his head down.

"Dovi?" a soft voice asked incredulously.

He stopped. It couldn't be. He looked up slowly, and there she was, one hand covering her mouth in surprise, the other resting loosely on the handlebar of Yair's stroller. The sun glinted off her diamond ring, and slowly a smile broke out across his face.

"Hi," he said softly.

"Hi," Gali answered, understanding dawning in her eyes.

And they turned and walked off together, as if they had arrived that way.

CHAPTER TWENTY-THREE

She glanced around at the circle of girls. It was like a children's birthday party gone wrong. Each chair was occupied by a client who looked like she'd rather be anywhere else in the world but there.

Well, this should be fun, Gali thought. She sat up straighter and clapped her hands. Eight sullen faces turned in her direction, all eyes hard and angry. Oh, boy.

She cleared her throat. "Why don't we go around the circle, and everyone can say one thing they've learned from Healthways so far?"

Eight pairs of eyes practically rolled in unison.

Gali sighed. Group sharing was not her favorite part of the day. And after this, she had a session with Aviva, who had recently left Healthways for some family matter and returned just last night.

Only Heaven knew what sort of condition the girl would be in after *that*. Gali really had no strength for games today...

"Okay, I'll go first." She leaned forward and crossed her legs, then uncrossed them. "Hi, I'm Gali. I've been a social worker in Healthways for seven years now, and the thing that I've really taken out of my time here is the fact that nothing is impossible. There is no situation that is too far gone, nothing broken so beyond repair that it can't be fixed. And that has really helped me on a daily basis. Thank you."

She leaned back and nodded to the girl next to her, while sneaking a look around the circle. *Okay, progress*, she thought with satisfaction. The pouts were gone, and now the expressions ranged from deathly bored to almost interested.

The girl whose turn it was crossed her arms and tilted her head to the side, sure signs of discomfort. "I'm Shiffy. Uh, what I learned so far is that I really hate having people watch me eat."

The girls all smiled, and thus began "the hate game": "I hate weighing myself in front of everybody." "I hate sharing a room." "I hate Healthways." "I hate therapy."

Gali rolled her eyes at their eloquence, but at least they were sharing...

SHE APPROACHED THE PINK DOOR once more, her heart hammering in trepidation. Aviva had gone home for two weeks, against all staff wishes. Now she had returned, and Gali was truly afraid to find out how the time spent outside of Healthways had affected the young girl. All sorts of scenarios ran through her mind, dizzying her with varying degrees of deterioration. But this wasn't helping. She forced her mind to go blank and knocked on the door.

Silence. Then, "Come in." The voice was neutral enough, and Gali entered.

The room was airy and bright, the bed was neatly made, and homey pictures were hanging on the walls.

Gali blinked. Was she in the wrong room? But there was Aviva, relaxing in an armchair, holding a book, and watching Gali's bewilderment with an amused expression on her face.

"Are you okay?" Aviva asked, a laugh filling her voice.

Gali sat down on the bed. "I'm fine, *baruch Hashem*. How are *you*?" she asked, careful not to make assumptions.

Aviva closed her book and looked Gali square in the face. Gali studied her. Her eyes were a clear blue, her skin looked fresh, her lips were unchapped, and her hair seemed less brittle. She wasn't the picture of good health, but she no longer seemed qualified to be the poster child for anorexia nervosa, either.

"I'm...doing really well," Aviva said thoughtfully. "*Baruch Hashem*," she added.

Gali smiled. "I'm so glad to hear." She *was* glad Aviva seemed so much better, but she was wary of the sudden change. "Would you like to go for a walk?" she asked the girl, observing her expression carefully.

Aviva looked at Gali, her eyes laughing. "You're trying to figure out what's different, aren't you?" she asked her, smiling knowingly.

Gali sat back, her face open. "You got me," she said. "Care to share?" She made her body language as unthreatening as possible, laying her hands loosely in her lap.

Aviva leaned forward, her face now serious. "Well, I went home for my brother's *yahrtzeit*..." Her voice faltered for a moment, and then she continued. "He was only seven, you know? It was the first year he was allowed to ride the bus by himself… He was going to visit our grandparents, and then…" She stopped, her eyes filling. "He was only seven," she said again, and Gali felt a sob catch in her own throat. She forced it back, imagining her college professor's look of disapproval as he intoned, "Keep your emotions in check, ladies. Create a barometer for yourselves to check if you are getting too emotional. Keep it on hand at all times." Gali used his advice often, although she didn't know how anybody could not feel emotional upon hearing about the murder of a little boy. But she forced herself to remain expressionless as she waited for Aviva to continue.

"We went to his *kever*, all of us together, as a family. And everyone was crying and *davening*, and I was just…quiet. Then, out of nowhere, there was this voice in my head, and it kept repeating the same words." She stopped and looked at Gali steadily. Gali looked back, her expression encouraging.

Aviva swallowed. "It said…'I don't want to die.'" A tear ran down her cheek, and she quickly brushed it away. "Nati didn't have a choice. But I do. I can live, if I choose to. And I do. I want to live. For Nati. For me. I don't want to die." She leaned back in her chair and curled up her legs. "That's why I came back. So you can all help me." She smiled at Gali's careful mask of emotions. "I want to finish this book now, if that's okay," she said, opening the book on her lap again. "Maybe I'll take you up on that walk later."

Gali recognized her dismissal. She got up from the bed, smoothed down her skirt, and walked toward the door. When she reached it, she turned back. "Aviva," she said softly. The girl looked up. "I'm really glad you came back."

The girl smiled, and Gali left.

SHE REACHED FOR THE RATTLE and jiggled it in the baby's face. He giggled, and she giggled with him. She was sitting on the rug in the living room, playing with Yair, her mind empty of everything except the joy of playing with this delicious baby.

She'd gone over Aviva's story a thousand times on the bus, turning it this way and that, trying to plan out her next move. Aviva had seemed completely genuine, but it wasn't common for someone to change so drastically, so quickly.

She had put all that aside the moment she had scooped Yair out of his crib and sent Dovi to take a nap. The poor guy was exhausted from being a stay-at-home father, and besides, if he napped, it gave them less time to discuss the elephant in the room.

They still hadn't come to an agreement about their Pesach plans. But after Dovi had told her how he had refused to remove his yarmulke the other day, she'd been going around with new seeds of hope sprouting in her heart. It was like Rabbi Gordon had told her: Dovi wasn't completely gone. Her Dovi, the *masmid* and *ben Torah* she had married, he was still there, buried beneath a mountain of pain and anger. She wasn't going to give up on him. She wasn't going to give up on her dreams of going to America for Pesach, either, though. She sighed.

Gali's phone rang just then. She was tempted to ignore it; this was family time, after all, and she'd had enough talking to people at work. She glanced at the screen, finger already hovering over the "ignore" button, when she saw the name. *Bracha Grossberg.*

Her heart rate sped up, and her hands started to shake. She

answered the call. "Hello?" She tried to sound confident and cheerful, but the tremor in her voice was unmistakable.

"Gali!" Bracha's warm voice rang out loudly. "How *are* you? How's little Yair doing?"

Gali tried to answer as naturally as possible, and the two women chatted about the baby's progress for a few minutes, though Gali felt she would burst at any moment from all the nervous suspense.

Finally, Bracha got to the point. "Gali, I'm calling to tell you that Shoshana has been asking about the baby. She is *not* ready to resume her role as mother yet, but she would like to visit you and check up on him. I told her that it was entirely up to you..." She let the question dangle while Gali tried to breathe.

Her mind whirled, imagining Shoshana, Yair's *real* mother, here, in her house. She was overcome with the childish desire to scream, "No! He's mine!" and slam down the phone. But since she wasn't five and Yair *wasn't* hers, she answered calmly, "I see. Well, let me talk to my husband, and I'll get back to you." She thanked Bracha and hung up.

Her husband. She said she'd speak to her husband. But what would Shoshana see if she came? She'd entrusted her baby to a nice *yeshivishe* couple, not one where the husband was plagued by *emunah* questions and suddenly didn't seem to know himself.

Gali scooped up Yair and held him close. She rubbed her cheek against the soft fuzz of his head and listened to his breathing.

"You like it here, don't you, sweetie?" she murmured. She tried to imagine life without him, but it was too depressing. Bracha had said Shoshana wasn't ready to take him back yet, but what if she wouldn't like what she saw at the Rothmans and would decide to entrust him to someone else?

Gali shuddered. She needed a listening ear, and Dovi always knew what to say. Besides, this decision needed to be made by both of them. She gave Yair one more hug and then went to wake up Dovi.

CHAPTER TWENTY-FOUR

He sat up groggily. "What time is it?" he croaked.

"Four o'clock," Gali whispered.

Dovi yawned. "Why are you whispering if you already woke me?" he asked crankily. Gali wrinkled her nose at him, and he felt bad. "Sorry, you know I'm in poor form after naps. What's up?" He leaned back against the headboard and grabbed a throw pillow from the armchair nearby.

Gali sat down in the armchair, hugging the baby close to her. Yair squirmed, wanting to be released from her tight grip. She put him down on the rug and then took her seat again. "Shoshana wants to come visit," she told Dovi grimly.

"Ohana who?" he asked around a giant yawn.

"Shoshana Weiss, Yair's mother!"

His eyebrows sprang up. "Oh," he said.

She lowered her eyes. "Bracha Grossberg, Shoshana's sister, just called to let me know this. I said I'd call her back. What do you think?"

Dovi looked at her. "What do *you* think?" he asked. She was silent. "Gali, if it's too much for you, I have no problem calling her back and telling her no. She'll understand, and besides, she's kind of in our debt right now. We can just say we think it would be bad for Yair, and she wouldn't be able to argue."

Gali listened, but she wasn't really hearing him. All she heard was "*my* baby, *my* baby, *my* baby," playing a fast staccato in time to her racing heart.

"Gali?" Dovi said gently.

She looked at him, hating the tears that were threatening to fall. When had she become so weepy? She used to be so strong and stoic, yet these days the tiniest wind seemed to reduce her to tears.

Dovi looked angry. "This is what I was afraid of," he said loudly, rubbing his forehead. "That taking in Yair would cause you pain! I was right. Look at you! You look like you are about to collapse! That's it; I'm calling Mrs. Grossberg right n—"

"No!" Gali burst out. "Don't!" She took a deep breath. "Don't call her! And don't ever say that you regret taking in Yair! He's part of our family now! He's ours, even if it's only for a little longer." She stopped abruptly and crouched on the floor next to the baby. He gurgled up at her and rolled onto his stomach, and then rolled again onto his back. This was his latest trick.

"I'll tell Bracha that Shoshana can come. He is her baby, after all. I could never stop a mother from seeing her baby..." She scooped up Yair, mumbled something incoherent to Dovi, and left the room.

He sat there, staring after her. "Well, I'm glad I could help," he mumbled. He wasn't really sure why she had come to him if she was just going to follow her own ideas anyway, but he was glad she had worked it out.

Dovi rubbed his head again. He needed a shower, and then he needed some coffee — in that order — and he had less than an hour until he was supposed to meet Avrami at the shul hall, where they would be cooking for the Friedman bar mitzvah. He flopped back down onto his pillows, feeling like a schoolboy hitting snooze on his alarm clock in the morning. He wasn't in the mood to be the jovial chef. Right now, he wanted to be the grumpy guy who stays in bed and forgets the world. He closed his eyes, enjoying the temporary darkness. Dark felt right. Dark was where he was comfortable...

He heard Yair cry, and he scrunched his forehead against the noise. He loved Yair. He loved the tiny kid so much that it was a physical feeling, but he couldn't think about himself. For the past few months, when it came to everything else, that was all he had done, but when it came to Yair, he was entirely focused on how fostering would make Gali feel. He tried to imagine what it would be like when this Shoshana wasn't merely coming for a visit, but rather to take her baby back, but all he saw was Gali's stricken face, and he felt his stomach turn, knowing there was nothing he could do to stop Gali's pain. He felt like roaring, like ripping open the pillow he still held and watching the feathers pour out in a vindictive shower...

His eyes popped open. That was a weird thought. Maybe he was losing it?

Eh, would it really make a difference? he wondered. He felt half-mad most of the time, anyway...

And with that cheerful thought, he went off to take a shower.

৯

HE FINISHED WRAPPING the last asparagus bits in phyllo dough, sprayed the whole lot with olive oil, and started putting the trays into the shul's large oven. Gali's kitchen was gorgeous, but it wasn't exactly made to fit one hundred appetizers in the oven at once. He sank into a chair and put his feet up. Avrami was running late, and Dovi was pretty sure it had something to do with his daughters. But ever since Gali's frenzied accusations in the kitchen that Friday night, Dovi felt a weird, prickly feeling every time Avrami spoke about his kids, so he avoided discussing them with him at all costs.

The truth was, they were already in a weird place after Dovi had lost the restaurant opportunity for them, although, surprisingly, Avrami hadn't mentioned it again. It was as if he knew that he'd pushed Dovi too far, and that if he wanted them to remain friends, it would be best not to remind Dovi of what had happened.

Dovi got up to pour a drink for himself and then sat back down. He pulled out his latest self-help book, *How to Know If You're Really Happy*, by John M. Rubio, opened up to his bookmark, and read, "Chapter Four: Getting to Know You." Dovi munched on some leftover asparagus and sipped his drink, his brows furrowed in concentration.

He read further: "Do you have a clear sense of who you are, what you want to achieve, and how you're going to achieve it?" He looked up, his eyes raking over the room as he thought. He used to know who he was. He used to know exactly who he was. But today, there was a stranger looking back at him from the reflection on the oven door. He stared at it morosely, until a voice behind him made him jump.

"Don't you know a watched oven never cooks, bro?"

Dovi turned and gave Avrami a small smile. "You finally made it here," he said, avoiding the whole staring-into-the-oven thing.

Avrami hung his bag on the hook next to the door. "Yeah," he said. That was it. No snide joke, witty remark, or inappropriate comment. Dovi looked at him sharply, but Avrami had started chopping onions for the creamy mushroom soup, and Dovi honestly didn't want to know anything else he might add.

Once the appetizers were cooling, the soup was bubbling, and Avrami was making the stuffed cabbage by himself — punishment for being late — Dovi pulled out his book again. He read, "Does the future look bright, and are you grateful for the present?"

Once again, the answers would have to be no and no. Well, he was grateful to be alive, sure, and he was grateful every day for Gali, but everything else pretty much belonged in the "terrible, horrible, no good, pretty bad day" book that he used to read as a child. In fact, the past six months seemed to him like one long, terrible, horrible, no good, pretty bad day.

He sighed and looked up to find Avrami smirking at him. "What?" he snapped.

Avrami put on a Gemara singsong. "If Dovi thinks that he will find answers in some ridiculous book, then Dovi is a *shoteh*."

Dovi threw an oven mitt at him. "And where do *you* look for answers, O Brilliant One? Bar Alley?" He snorted.

Avrami deftly wrapped up the last cabbage leaf. "Ah, that is the difference between you and me, Dovi bear. You want answers. I want silence. I want alcohol and music to block out all the screeching voices in my head. You, my friend, want to embrace those voices. You want to clarify things for them. Well, guess what? You're losing the battle. I see you, and I see that no matter how hard you search, you can't seem to make sense of anything anymore. And pretty soon, you're going to put down your silly books and that fancy flute of yours, and you'll accept my mindset, too."

Dovi stared at him.

"Okay, done the cabbage," Avrami said brightly. "Should we move on to the sweet potato soufflé?"

Dovi nodded mutely.

"Oh, don't look so sad, Dovs," Avrami said softly. "You're breaking my heart."

Dovi gave a half-smile. "You don't have a heart. And I'm just upset that it got so late, and we still have to make three side dishes and a dessert. Now, move, please," he said briskly.

And as he fried green beans with cherry tomatoes and seasoned the spinach-potato wedges, he tried to forget about the book. But the question "Does the future look bright?" kept playing in his head while his knife thunked out potato chunks with the final beat of *no, no, no.*

CHAPTER TWENTY-FIVE

She straightened the painting and stepped back to look. Hmm, now it leaned too far to the right. She pushed it, and stepped back again. Perfect. She stared at the painting for a moment, taking in the relaxing pond and meadow scene.

She remembered the day they'd bought it. It had been almost seven years ago. They'd just left the doctor's office, and the future looked grim. Five years of childlessness, and the medical staff of flesh and blood could offer her no hope. She and Dovi had walked along in silence, heads bent against the wind, wrapped up in silent worlds of private pain, when it began to rain. They had run under the awning of a nearby strip of stores, including an art gallery, and Gali could taste the salt on her face, and she knew that the weather had loosened her last vestiges of self-control, and that her tears were now mixing with the raindrops.

She'd turned around quickly, not wanting Dovi to see that she was crying. And then, facing the storefront of the art gallery, she'd suddenly discovered this painting.

"Dovi, look!" she'd whispered, pointing at the canvas on display in the window. A meadow of lush greens and yellows sprawled across the painting, meeting the perfect blue sky and touching on a crystal-clear pond. Fish could be seen in the pond's depths, and flowers were peeking up around its edges. It was a painting of the perfect day.

Gali had pressed her face to the window glass, mesmerized. That was where she wanted to be right then. She wanted to sit on a rock, dangle her feet in the pond, and feel the sun's caress on her forehead. She wanted to leave behind the pain, the despair, the wind, and the rain, even if just for a second.

She'd heard the jingle of bells and had straightened up, startled. Dovi had entered the store. She looked out at the street, at the rain's angry litany, at the mud forming alongside the roads, and she felt more alone than she'd ever felt before. Then Dovi was back, and he was grinning.

"Here," he'd said, presenting her with a small receipt.

Confused, she'd stretched out a cold hand and looked at it. Then she looked at Dovi. "You bought it," she stated. It wasn't a question.

He nodded happily. "They said they'll frame it and deliver it later today!"

Gali stared at the receipt again. "But it cost a fortune!"

Dovi shrugged. "We can afford it." He gave a little smile, and she offered a tremulous one in return.

"Come," Dovi said, reaching out and flagging down a passing cab.

At that minute, the sun broke through the clouds, chasing away the rain. Gali threw back her hood and felt the sun caress her forehead. Then she'd followed Dovi into the cab…

Gali stood there, lost in memories, until Yair gave an angry whimper.

She started. "Oh, coming, sweetie pie!" she called, going over to the crib and lifting him out. "Did you wake up?" she cooed. She checked his diaper and then put him down on the play-mat with his pacifier.

She needed to finish straightening up. Shoshana would be there in half an hour! Gali dusted the bookshelf, fluffed the couch cushions, and brought out a platter of brownies and a pitcher of water.

Dovi ambled in just then wearing sweatpants and a hooded sweatshirt. He must have seen the look of horror on her face, because he chuckled dryly and said, "Don't worry, I'm changing," and ambled out.

She sighed deeply and scooped up Yair. He looked adorable in his light-blue knit leggings and a cream knit top. She pulled a little hat over his head, and he gurgled. She giggled despite her nervousness and went to check her own reflection. She looked pretty, but did she look like a competent, warm, and nurturing foster mother? Hmm, well, she hoped so. She sat down on the couch and played with the baby's toes until Dovi joined her.

She stopped herself from gasping out loud, but tears filled her eyes. It was the old Dovi, Dovi the *yeshivah yungerman*. He wore a black velvet yarmulke, a white button-down shirt, black pants, and black shoes, and his *tzitzis* hung loosely at his sides. She felt a pang of longing that she instantly tried to squash.

But he knew her too well for that. "You miss this, don't you?" he asked, sitting beside her on the couch. She heard the wistful note in his voice, and she understood that he was the one who missed it. Not the dress, per se, but rather being the fulfillment of her hopes and dreams.

Before she could say anything in response, the doorbell rang.

A whole family of butterflies burst out of their cocoons in Gali's stomach, and she found herself squeezing Yair.

"Too tight," she heard Dovi say, and she quickly loosened her grip on the baby.

"Sorry, my little boy," she whispered to Yair as Dovi went to answer the door.

"Welcome," she heard Dovi say warmly, and then there she was, a small blond woman, a girl, really, probably a little younger than Gali, thirty years old at the most. She looked just like Chaviva, but there was no sparkle in her emerald eyes, and the bags under them sagged with what seemed like the weight of the world.

Gali jumped to her feet, holding Yair securely, and smiled at her visitor. "Hi, please come in," she said softly. "Sit down. Can I pour you a drink?"

Shoshana nodded and sank into an armchair gratefully. "Some water, please," she said.

As she drank, Gali felt herself grow nauseous from nerves. Then Shoshana put down the cup. "May I?" she asked suddenly, gesturing at the baby.

Gali felt herself grow hot and then cold, and her arms tightened around the baby once more. "No!" she wanted to shout. But Shoshana was staring at her, and Dovi was silently begging her, and so —

"Of course!" she heard herself exclaim, and she held out the baby and placed him into Shoshana's small hands.

Shoshana adjusted him expertly and gazed down at her child. Gali looked away, at her painting on the wall, and found herself longing, once more, to jump into it and never come back out.

"He's beautiful," Shoshana murmured. "He looks just like his siblings." She hefted the baby into one arm and removed a picture from her bag, handing it to Gali.

Gali took it. Six smiling kids gazed back at her, some blond, some dark, and all with the same green eyes. Gali thought of her own dark eyes, and she felt a pang of pain. Yair obviously wasn't hers.

She mentally copied and pasted his face into the picture, right next to the smallest child, a little dark-haired girl with curls and green eyes. He fit perfectly. She looked up to see Shoshana watching her, her expression unreadable. She handed back the picture.

"So how is he doing?" Shoshana asked, suddenly brisk.

Gali leaned forward. "He's doing amazing, *baruch Hashem*. The pediatrician says he's developing wonderfully, and we...we adore him," she said hoarsely, begging herself not to cry.

Shoshana glanced at her — and was that pity in her gaze? "Here," she said, handing the baby back to Gali, who grasped his warm weight like a drowning person grabbing at a rope. "You are obviously doing an amazing job."

Shoshana got to her feet. She walked to the door, Gali and Dovi bobbing along in her wake. "Thank you," she added, turning suddenly.

Gali took a startled step back. "Of course," she said softly. The two women gazed at each other for a moment.

"*Simchos*," Shoshana wished her, and just like that, she was gone.

Gali followed Dovi back into the living room, and suddenly she was crying, a blinding torrent of tears cascading down her face. Dimly, she felt Dovi take the baby from her arms as she sank onto the couch, sobbing into the fluffed cushion as the sun made shadows on the painting of a meadow and a pond on her wall.

CHAPTER TWENTY-SIX

She slammed her cup down. Coffee splashed over the rim of the mug, forming a small puddle on the marble countertop. She looked down at the liquid pooling and felt a pang of regret. Dovi remained silent as Gali went to get a paper towel. She wiped up the coffee, wishing she could just as easily clean away the argument she was having with her husband, yet again.

Gali remembered the days, not so long ago, when Dovi was the only person who she felt truly understood her in the big, lonely world that had become her life. But today he was aggravating her with his stubbornness. His insistence might have stemmed from many things, but clearheadedness was certainly not one of them.

She ground her teeth together, sent up a silent prayer for success, and tried again. "Dovi. The man asked you to take off your yarmulke.

He's...*l'toeles*, let's just say I don't think he's a good person. Now how in the world do you still want to spend time with him?!" She was so distressed, she was tripping over her words.

"Gali, Avrami is not a bad guy," Dovi said staunchly, his face serious. "He's just confused. And so am I. So what makes us so different? Unless...you think I'm 'not a good person' too?" He stared at her, and she felt her mouth drop open from shock and hurt.

"Dovi!" she gasped. "How can you even say that?!"

But it was too late. Dovi had already left the room.

ॐ

GALI TRIED TO EMPTY HER MIND of all thoughts of home and family as she entered the Healthways office. If she wanted to give her clients her all, she needed to leave her own life behind the minute she stepped through the big arched doorway of the clinic.

She straightened her shoulders, took off her sunglasses, and smoothed down her blue flared skirt. She walked over to the secretary and smiled.

"Good morning, Zeesi," she said brightly. "Do you have my schedule ready?"

Zeesi groaned. "How in Heaven's name are you always so chirpy in the morning?" she asked, rifling around her desk for Gali's timetable. "I can barely string together two nice words, and here you are, so cheerful and..." She stopped, trying to think of just the right word. "Shiny," she concluded. "Cheerful and shiny." She handed Gali her schedule.

Gali laughed. "I have no idea what you mean by that, but I'll take it as a compliment," she called over her shoulder as she left the office. She wondered if Zeesi would still think she was so "shiny" if she'd seen her argue with her husband this morning. She sighed and looked down at her schedule.

10:00: Supervise breakfast

11:00: Morning weigh-in

1:00: Settle in two new members

2:00: Session with Aviva

Gali smiled as she thought of the girl who used to cause her so much angst. Aviva was doing really well, *baruch Hashem*. The rest of the staff at Healthways was dumbfounded by the girl's change, but Gali knew that Aviva was far from healed. There was still a long road ahead of her before she could make it on her own, but at least she now *wanted* to get well, and that made all the difference.

She made a quick phone call to the babysitter to check on Yair — they'd started sending him out when Dovi got busy with his catering business — and after hearing the babysitter's reassurance that Yair was cooing happily and playing with his toes, Gali hurried over to the dining room. Supervising thirty sullen teenagers eating breakfast was far from fun, but she knew it was a vital part of the therapy program. There had to be full supervision at all times, and personalized meal plans for each client.

She kept a watchful eye on the girls as she laid out two case files in front of her. She needed to prepare before settling in the new girls. She opened the first folder and glanced around the room. Everyone seemed to be cooperating; most girls were still half-asleep, their eyes closing as they slowly spooned yogurt or cereal into their mouths. Satisfied, Gali glanced back down.

March 16, 2016: Patient joins home.

Age: 14

Height: 5'3"

Weight: 92 lb.

Family Situation: Parents divorced. Father irreligious; mother lives in New York with two brothers. Patient recently moved to Israel with father and sister. Patient has unhealthy relationship with father; suspicions of abuse are evident. Referred to Healthways by previous social worker.

Patient Status: Moderate anorexia nervosa. Healthways is her first clinic.

Gali felt herself break out in goosebumps. Something about this profile sounded suspiciously familiar. She was almost scared to look at the patient's name. Her eyes traveled slowly up the page...and there it was: *Ora Meyers*, in solid black letters.

Gali felt her stomach drop. She was suddenly lightheaded and dizzy, and there was a faint ringing sound in her ears. The line, *suspicions of abuse*, suddenly floated across her mind, and she heard the echoes of Dovi's argument that morning: *He's not a bad guy, Gali...*

Not a bad guy...not a bad guy...suspicions of abuse... Gali thought she was going to be sick. She laid her head in her hands and breathed deeply.

Dimly she heard the sounds of a commotion, and she looked up. Natalia had burst into tears and was trying to spill her yogurt down the sink drain while her friends wrestled with her. Gali jumped to her feet and ran over to intervene, all thoughts of Ora Meyers rushing from her mind. After convincing Natalia to eat her yogurt and sending her off to meet with her counselor, Gali walked into the staff room, her hands shaking. It was turning out to be quite a morning.

She poured herself a cup of water and sat down, sipping it slowly. There was so much to process here! Firstly, she had been right on the mark about Ora having an eating disorder. Secondly, she was now to be Ora's counselor, which might make things harder on the poor girl. Gali toyed with the idea of passing her over to another therapist, but she promptly squelched the notion. Everything happened for a reason, and if Hashem wanted her to help Ora, then help her she would.

The third glaring fact was...Avrami Meyers seemed to be abusing Ora. In what way, she wasn't sure. But whatever it was, Gali was going to get to the bottom of it. And when she was done, and the suspicions proved to be true, pigs were going to be flying before Avrami Meyers was allowed anywhere near his daughters — or Dovi — again.

She looked up as a smiling Rachel walked into the room.

"Hey, Gali. Tough morning?" Rachel greeted her. She snatched up an apple and recited a *brachah* loudly and clearly.

Gali answered amen and then let her head thunk down on the table. "I've had better ones," she said, her voice muffled.

Rachel laughed. "Oh, c'mon, it can't be that bad, can it?"

Gali didn't lift her head. "You'd be surprised," was all she said.

Rachel was quiet. "Anything I can do?" she finally asked.

Gali heard a noise. She looked up to find Rachel sitting right next to her, her face a mask of concern.

Gali smiled. "You're so sweet. Okay, have you ever opened a case file and realized you already know the client?"

Rachel smiled. "Ah, every therapist's nightmare come true. Well, the answer is yes. Five years ago, I opened up my case file, and lo and behold, it was a relative of my husband's! I thought I was going to throw up. There were all these details about her private life, things I couldn't 'un-know.' And we got together a lot, at Chanukah parties and *melaveh malkahs*... It was awful. But it ended up turning out okay. I helped her through a lot, and I think she would never have opened up to a complete stranger. Today, she's a totally functioning mother with three children..." Her voice trailed off as Gali straightened up.

"So you're saying I shouldn't worry?" she asked hopefully.

Rachel gave her a wry smile. "I'm saying you should worry tons, actually. But I'm also saying that Hashem gave you this client for a reason, and it's up to you to do your best."

Gali leaned over and gave her friend a hug. "Thanks, Rachel. You're the best. Oh no, I'm late for weigh-in!" She jumped up. "I need to run. Thanks for the talk! I'll catch you later."

She ran out of the room and walked briskly toward the weigh-in room, her mind whirring. Right now, she had to weigh thirty girls. Maybe after that she'd have the courage to face Avrami Meyers's daughter.

CHAPTER TWENTY-SEVEN

Sometimes a moment can be so much more than just that. To an outsider, there is merely a desk, a chair, and a client, but in reality, there's a long chain of dominoes that will crash into each other, wreaking havoc as they fall, if just given that first, tiny push...

These thoughts flitted through her mind as she stared across the desk at Ora Meyers. How she wished the girl would just speak. The anticipation of it all was making her sick. She glanced subtly down at her phone, where the words "four missed calls" were flashing. Dovi had tried to call her, but she hadn't picked up. She couldn't! What was she supposed to say? "Hey, Dovi, how was your morning? By the way, your new best friend is an abuser, and he is destroying his older daughter. Do you mind getting some milk for the house?" She sighed, just a little too loudly, and the sound filled the small room. Finally, just as she was about to break her own rule and speak first, Ora cleared her throat.

"This is pretty weird, huh?" she asked, fingering the bangles around her wrist.

Gali's heart went out to her; who knew what kind of horrors the poor girl had been through? But she kept her emotions in check. She smiled and leaned back in her chair. "Why do you say that?" she asked, watching Ora's face closely.

The girl smirked. "You know. One second I'm your Shabbos guest; the next, I'm lying on your couch, spilling my guts out."

Gali smiled at this. "So far, no couches and no guts, so maybe not that weird, hmm?"

Ora looked down. "I guess..." She stared around the room, her eyes landing on the folders on Gali's desk. "Do you have one of me?" she asked, pointing her chin at the pile.

Gali gazed at the girl steadily. "I do," she said honestly. "Does that bother you?"

Ora shrugged. "Not really. Mrs. Plotnick, my old counselor, you know, from Brooklyn, would practically write down every time I sneezed. I'm used to it."

Gali smiled at the exaggeration, but something was niggling at her. *Mrs. Plotnick, my old counselor...from Brooklyn...* Where had Gali recently heard about a counselor named Plotnick from Brooklyn...?

Oh, at the conference! Gali suddenly remembered. Adele Plotnick had been the social worker from Brooklyn, New York...who had the adolescent client whose father was her worst nightmare! It just *had* to be Ora Meyers.

Gali sat up straight as the pieces all fell into place. She was awed by Hashem's *hashgachah*.

Adele Plotnick had asked her all about Healthways at the conference, and she'd seemed impressed with their work. It occurred to Gali that Adele was probably the one who had referred Ora to them once she found out that Ora would be moving to Israel. That meant that if Gali wouldn't have attended that conference, Adele Plotnick might not have sent Ora to Healthways...and then Gali might never have received actual proof as to the kind of man Avrami Meyers really was.

She leaned forward, her hands flat out on the desk in a physical display of candor. "Ora, I would like to ask you a question."

The girl looked resigned. "Shoot," she said, flicking her long red hair over her shoulder.

Gali looked her in the eye, weighing each word carefully. "Why are you here?" she asked.

Ora didn't miss a beat. "Because I have an eating disorder," she said matter-of-factly.

Gali mentally penned "not in denial" in Ora's folder and then leaned forward again. "Another question."

Ora exhaled loudly. "I didn't think it was going to be just one."

Gali didn't smile back. "Ora, do you know how — or rather, why — your eating disorder developed?"

Ora stared at her, her eyes suddenly cold and dark. Gali wanted to look away, uncomfortable to be prying into this girl's private world of pain, but she didn't dare. The clock on top of Ora's head ticked loudly. Ora fiddled with her bangles, their clinking in sync with the ticking of the clock, until the room seemed to be filled with all sorts of sounds, except for the voices of its occupants.

Then, just when Gali was about to despair of Ora answering her question, the clinking stopped.

"Yes, I think so," the girl said quietly. "It's...because of my father."

⇗

THINGS WERE OUT OF CONTROL. Out. Of. Control. Gali sighed as she pushed open the door to her apartment. The house seemed quiet. Too quiet. Dovi should have picked up Yair from the babysitter an hour ago. Where were they?

"Hello?" she called hesitantly, wandering into the kitchen. A note was taped onto the fridge. She pulled it off and read: *Gali, tried to call you. Work emergency, dropped off Yair at Mrs. Larsky across the street. We are doing a last-minute bar mitzvah in Netanya. Be back late. Sorry about the inconvenience. Dovi.*

Gali could practically feel his hurt wafting off of the page. He obviously hadn't gotten over their argument from that morning. But what bothered her more was the "we" he had used: *We are doing a last-minute bar mitzvah.* That meant Dovi...and Ora Meyers's father. Ora had refused to divulge what exactly her father was doing to her, but the fact that she'd admitted that there was something about their relationship that had caused her anorexia to develop, was enough proof to Gali that Avrami Meyers was truly up to no good. Now, reading Dovi's note, Gali felt sick. Her husband — sweet, innocent, good Dovi — was out of town with a dangerous criminal.

Grabbing her cell phone, she punched in Dovi's number. It rang five times before he picked up.

"Hello?" he said, his voice distant.

"Dovi," she gasped, her voice trembling. "Dovi...come home." She was almost sobbing.

His voice changed in an instant. "What's wrong?" he asked sharply. "Is it Yair? Are you okay? Did something happen?"

Gali stopped. *Yes!* she wanted to scream. *Something* did *happen! And it's harmful for Yair and for me! You brought a sick man into our midst, and now you are allowing him to pull you away from all that you used to hold dear. Your* Yiddishkeit, *your family, yourself!*

But she couldn't tell him this. She wasn't able to. Patient confidentiality was no small matter, and besides, she would have to ask a *she'eilah* before divulging such private information. But in the meantime, her husband, her baby's foster father, was rubbing shoulders with the scum of the earth! And she was powerless to stop him.

"No," she said quietly. "Nothing happened. I just...want you to come home."

There was silence on the line, and then Dovi spoke, sounding just as distant as before. "I'll be home later," he said quietly. "Bye, Gali." And the phone went dead.

Gali stared down at the screen, at the words "call ended," and she felt the tears begin. What was she supposed to do? Break the law, break her client's trust, but get her husband away from Avrami Meyers? Or keep her word, be a good, law-abiding social worker, and allow her husband to drift further and further away, while she stayed behind, trying desperately to hold together all the pieces of her life that were slowly unraveling?

She cried and cried, allowing the hurt to leave her, to spill out onto the countertop, to soak her sleeves with their salty stream. And then, when she was empty and raw, she went into the other room, took out a Tehillim, and turned her pain into prayers.

CHAPTER TWENTY-EIGHT

Spring was just around the corner. The days were getting longer, the sun was shining in the pristine blue sky, and the air smelled of fresh grass, trees, and flower blossoms. Life would have been perfect, if it weren't for the fact that winter seemed to have taken up permanent residence in her home, turning everything frosty and cold. Dovi was barely speaking to her, Yair had the sniffles, and Gali seemed to have lost her usual zest for life. Sometimes, she thought as she wrote up a list of whom they needed to send *mishloach manos* to, she felt like just giving up. Why did everything have to be so *hard*? No one else seemed to find it hard to have children, a normal family. No one else seemed to find it hard to have a G-d-fearing husband. No one else seemed to find it hard to go to work, to face the people there. But for Gali, none of these things were effortless. And she didn't know why.

She went to make the *kreplach* for the Purim *seudah*. Dovi had invited a few *shanah aleph* boys from the yeshivah — they had no clue what Dovi was going through now, only that he had taken a break from his position in their yeshivah — and Gali had invited Rachel and her family for the *seudah*, as well.

She rolled out the dough methodically, her mind racing. She hadn't had a one-on-one session with Ora since that first introductory one, but she'd seen the girl at weigh-in and at lunch yesterday. Ora had smiled at her during lunch and had scowled at her during weigh-in, so Gali wasn't really sure where their relationship stood. She had felt like the girl trusted her during their conversation, but she still hadn't revealed the extent of her father's abuse.

Gali tasted the bile that always rose while thinking of Avrami Meyers. She went to wash her hands, and then quickly peeked in at the baby. Poor thing was sleeping with his mouth open, and he was snoring like an old man. She giggled as he frowned in his sleep. He brought her so much joy...but she knew his days as her baby were numbered. Yair was almost half a year old. Two or three more months, and he would be back with Shoshana, his real mother, and his six siblings.

"Why does she need so many?" she asked aloud, childishly. She leaned over Yair and inhaled his sweet, milky scent. "She has seven *bli ayin hara*, and I have none. I think, fair is fair; I should get to keep one." She looked around quickly to make sure Dovi hadn't overheard her musings as they veered into the boundaries of kidnapping. She sighed, then went back into the kitchen to pour herself a cup of juice.

What was *wrong* with her? What had happened to the cool and collected woman she used to be? That woman had been so at peace with her lot in life... When had she turned into such a whiner? She laughed bitterly, remembering how she had counseled a client yesterday, stressing again and again the importance of positive thinking. What a hypocrite she'd become.

She drank her juice and looked up to find Dovi standing there, looking rather uncomfortable in his own kitchen.

"Hey, Dovs," she forced herself to say lightly. "There are brownies in that pan; help yourself."

"Thanks," he muttered, shuffling over. A few minutes later, he was perched on a bar stool, eating a brownie in awkward silence.

"Can I pour you a cup of milk?" she asked, trying to keep her tone neutral and non-accusing. "Thanks," he said again.

"Nice yarmulke," she responded, only half-sarcastically, pointing toward the B'tei'avon Catering logo on his yarmulke.

Dovi reached up and touched it self-consciously. "Oh, yeah," he said. "You hate it, don't you?" He raised an eyebrow.

"Only a little," she said, and suddenly they were both laughing.

Gali's shoulders heaved with mirth, and she allowed herself to forget all else in the simple enjoyment of the moment. Finally she wiped her eyes and gave one last chuckle. "Well, that felt good," she said.

Dovi looked down. "It did, didn't it?"

Gali nodded, suddenly not trusting herself to speak.

Dovi looked up, and there was something almost desperate about his expression. "Gali, I—" he started to say, when a sudden loud sneeze sounded from the other room, followed by Yair's cries.

"*Oy*, poor baby," Gali said as she got up and raced toward Yair. She didn't want to hear whatever long, convoluted apology Dovi had bursting out of him. If he wanted to disrupt their lives with his soul-searching, that was fine. But she didn't want to hear about how he regretted doing it. She wanted to believe he truly needed this whole journey he was taking in order to find peace and happiness, because then, maybe, one day she'd understand. But if he started being wishy-washy about ever needing this soul-searching business to begin with, she was afraid she would burst and tell him to just grow up, stop being a baby, accept the cards Hashem had dealt him, and drop the whole disturbance in their lives once and for all.

She gathered Yair up and gently wiped his dripping nose. "Poor little baby," she crooned, kissing him. He whimpered, and she snuggled into him.

Dovi came in, looking anxious. "Is he okay?"

"*Baruch Hashem*," she whispered. "Why don't you put him back to sleep, and I'll go finish the *kreplach*?" She handed him the baby.

He nodded, and she hurried back into the kitchen before he could say anything else.

ะ❧

THE MEN WERE SINGING DRUNKENLY, food and drink were spilling merrily, and Rachel's kids were all running around on sugar highs. Gali felt like her face was going to break from smiling so much. She just loved Purim.

Yair was in his infant seat, dressed like a snow-white bunny rabbit, with fluffy pink ears and a black little nose. He looked adorable, and all the kids kept coming over to tickle him so he would giggle.

"They love babies," Rachel said to Gali as they made platters of chicken wings at the kitchen table.

"Me too," Gali said softly, and there wasn't much to say after that.

They brought the food out to a resounding chorus of "*Shoshanas Yaakov*" and much table-banging and clapping. The women went to sit at the end of the table. She and Rachel tried to schmooze, but the men were making too much noise, so they just ate and attended to the kids in companionable silence.

The bell rang, and Gali excused herself to go answer the door.

"Rabbi Gordon!" she gasped, taking a step back to allow the prestigious guest into their home.

The *rosh yeshivah* bounded into the house, clearly inebriated, his face lit up. "I've come to see my Dovi'le!" he shouted exuberantly. "A *freilichen* Purim, Rebbetzin," he added, as he entered the dining room. Gali followed him in hesitantly.

At the sight of their beloved *rosh yeshivah*, the boys all stood up and began singing "*Ashrei Mi She'amalo BaTorah*." Soon a circle formed around the table as the men danced with obvious love and joy. But Rabbi Gordon was trying to reach Dovi.

"Dovi'le!" he cried, reaching out his hands.

"Rebbi!" Dovi shouted back, trying to break through the circle. He tugged at the enjoined hands, like a child trying to break through a Red Rover chain, and finally, he was free. "Rebbi!" he called again, and then he was by his side, sobbing on the great man's shoulder.

"Dovi," the *rosh yeshivah* said, patting him on the back. "Dovi, I came to tell you to come home! Come home to yeshivah, Dovi; it's where you belong!"

Dovi looked at his *rebbi*, his close mentor, and the tears started falling thick and fast down his face. "But it hurts, Rebbi!" he sobbed. "It hurts too much!"

And now Rabbi Gordon was crying, and Gali was crying, and the boys kept dancing, oblivious to the heartrending scene playing out in the corner of the dining room.

Rabbi Gordon took Dovi's hands in his and said softly, "Yes, sometimes life does hurt, Dovi'le, and we don't understand why. But Hashem sees your pain. He knows your breaking point — and He won't let you break. He won't let you fall. Because He loves you, Dovi. Never forget that. He loves you, and He's going to help you..."

He started swaying back and forth, still holding onto Dovi's hands. "*Afilu b'hastarah, sheb'soch hahastarah, b'vadai gam sham nimtza Hashem Yisbarach...*" *Even in the darkness, inside the darkness, Hashem is right there...* He sang on, his voice rising and falling in the bittersweet melody, as Dovi watched him, not joining in, but just staring through his tears.

"Sing, Dovi'le," Rabbi Gordon commanded, and so together they sang: "*Gam sham nimtza Hashem Yisbarach...*" The rest of the crowd slowly joined in as the day faded away and bright stars began to appear in the Jerusalem sky overhead.

CHAPTER TWENTY-NINE

Gali pulled at the zipper, hoping sheer will would close the suitcase, but so far, it wasn't working. She sat on top of it and bounced up and down, thinking her added weight would cause things to settle in flatter. When that didn't work, she gave up and flopped down on her bed, wiping her forehead. She still couldn't believe they were going to America for Pesach!

She smiled, thinking back to Motza'ei Purim, after all the guests had cleared out. "Must sleep," a drunken Dovi had muttered, stumbling off toward the couch. She'd run after him with a garbage pail, and told him to please use it if he felt sick.

"I'm serious, Dovi!" she said sternly. "These couches do not absorb well."

"Mmm-hmm," he'd acquiesced.

She'd sighed and gone into the kitchen to bring him some Advil and a cup of water. When she came back, he'd already fallen asleep. She'd put the water and pills down on the coffee table and started to leave the room, flicking off the light on her way out.

"Gali?" Dovi had suddenly murmured sleepily into the darkness, apparently not fully asleep.

She'd stopped, still facing the door. "Yes?"

"Gali, thank you for a great Purim... I'd really love to go with you to your parents for Pesach."

She'd frozen in her place. Had she heard him correctly?! Was he just speaking drunkenly, or was he actually serious?

But the next day, when his hangover had worn off, Dovi told her that yes, he truly *was* happy to go to Baltimore for Pesach. He'd play his role as the old Dovi for those couple of weeks, and it would be fine; she shouldn't feel guilty about the whole thing. Gali wasn't sure where his turnaround had come from, although she suspected it had something to do with Rabbi Gordon's visit on Purim, as Dovi had been oddly quiet since then. Whatever it was, she certainly wasn't going to question Dovi about it.

They were flying later this week, but Gali had wanted to get a head start on the packing, which was why she was trying to finish up with this suitcase now. She hated last-minute rushing around and always tried to alleviate unnecessary stress from traveling. Of course, they'd never traveled with a baby before, so she was pretty sure they would end up stressed either way, but she was too excited to care.

She left the bedroom, almost skipping into the kitchen. She turned on the surround sound system, and music flowed through the speakers. She sighed happily and went to pour herself a cup of coffee.

She was more than excited about the upcoming trip; she was exuberant. Who knew? Maybe Dovi would feel so comfortable slipping back into his old self that he would let the façade last even longer than the duration of the trip... And maybe, just maybe, that would include dropping Avrami Meyers as his friend...

Gali shuddered at the thought of the man and took a sip of the soothing brew. Ahhh. She needed this. Yair had woken up several times during the night, and she was exhausted. Not that she was able to sleep much lately, anyway. She had been tossing and turning, worrying about Ora and Avrami and Dovi, although it was, to be honest, unnecessary. She really knew what she needed to do: she had to go to Mrs. Rappaport and tell her that she was unable to continue counseling Ora. Period. She was much too emotionally involved in the whole situation, and she didn't think that was beneficial to anyone.

Dropping a client would be a first for her, and Gali hated the idea. Years of having no children to be preoccupied with had turned her into a super-focused and completely committed advocate for her clients, and she felt too responsible for them to ever want to give over their cases to anyone else. True, she was much more distracted now that she had Yair... Did that make her a less dedicated social worker? Perhaps that was why it had taken her so long to come to the conclusion that she could not continue working with Ora. But better late than never. She would request a meeting with the supervisor tomorrow, and that would settle things. She sighed and finished her coffee.

The phone rang as she was taking her mug over to the sink. "Hello?" she said distractedly, giving the mug a quick rinse.

"Gali? It's Bracha."

Gali dropped the cup. Thankfully, it didn't break. "Hello," she said shortly, not trusting herself to speak.

"How is Yair doing?" Bracha asked gently, sensing, perhaps, the panic that Gali was sure she was emitting.

"He's doing great, *baruch Hashem*," she answered, hoping Bracha couldn't hear the way her voice was shaking.

"I'm sure he is, from the way you take care of him," the older woman said kindly, and Gali felt an odd ringing in her ears. This was it. She knew it. She wished Bracha would just say it already, so she could hang up the phone and cry.

"Gali," Bracha started. She stopped, maybe hoping Gali would help her out, but Gali's tongue was stuck to the roof of her mouth, and there was a basketball-sized lump in her throat. "Shoshana is doing much better, *chasdei Hashem*," Bracha said finally. "She wants to have Yair back by Shavuos…"

Gali had been expecting this, but that still did not prepare her for the searing pain that rippled through her heart, paralyzing her with its intensity. She finished the conversation somehow and found herself sitting numbly on the couch.

Two and a half months. Yair would be leaving her in two and a half months.

She closed her eyes and tried to remember life before Yair had come, before his light had filled up her home. But all she could conjure up were dark, gray, fuzzy images of quiet rooms and lonely nights, and suddenly she was weeping. She sobbed as if she would never stop, the pain of twelve years of emptiness spilling out in one endless cry. She sank forward onto the cushions and let the cries emerge, as broken and shattered as her heart. She only fell silent when she heard the front door open. Dovi entered, pushing Yair's carriage ahead of him.

"Hello, Mommy Gali!" he said brightly. "We're home, and we're hungry!"

He stopped still at the look on Gali's face. "What?" he asked sharply.

So she told him.

CHAPTER THIRTY

She didn't want to leave Yair. Now that she knew exactly when he'd be rejoining his family, every second together with him had become even more precious. But what could she do? She had to go to work...

"Goodbye, my sweet baby," she murmured, kissing the top of his silken head. He gurgled and gave her a buck-toothed smile. He'd gotten his two front teeth in one shot, which was double the discomfort for him, but half the sleepless nights for Gali. Her sister Chana had reassured her that he would grow into his teeth one day. Not that she would see that happen, but it was still nice to know. Gali gave him one last squeeze, and then she handed him over to the babysitter and left.

She walked briskly to the bus stop, thinking about Dovi, who was on his way now to Ramot where he'd be catering a luncheon. Gali had decided it was better for her mental health when she pretended Dovi was working alone and that Avrami Meyers did not exist. Of course, as a social worker, she really should not be advocating denial, but in this case, she was making an exception.

She boarded her bus and took a seat in the back, keeping her sunglasses securely on her face as a subtle "do not disturb" sign. She needed to plan out exactly what she was going to say to Mrs. Rappaport regarding switching Ora Meyers to a different social worker. Uncomfortable as she was about the whole idea, she knew it would be best for everyone like this. Let someone else, someone who did not know Avrami Meyers, discover the extent of his abuse. Let someone who had not hosted Avrami and Ora for Shabbos figure out whether or not the authorities needed to be involved. Gali couldn't help secretly dreaming about having Avrami Meyers locked up in prison, far away from his daughters and — she might as well say it — from her husband, and she wondered whether that made her a bad person. No, she decided, it didn't make her a bad person; it just made her human.

The automated announcer proclaimed her stop, and she got off the bus, still trying to formulate a plan. Mrs. Rappaport was an extremely straight shooter, and did not believe in allowing personal feelings to get in the way of professionalism. On the other hand, she was completely committed to her clients and only wanted what was best for them. Gali had already reached the building, and the only plan she'd come up with was to simply tell her the truth. She wouldn't start spilling out her trouble with Dovi, of course; after all, a little dignity was required. But she would explain that the case was just too close to home...

"Hi, Zeesi," she greeted the secretary. She walked to the cooler and poured herself a cup of water, bringing one over to Zeesi as well.

"Oh, thanks, Gali!" Zeesi threw her a grateful smile. "Mrs. Rappaport is expecting you; just go on in." She pointed at the supervisor's office door with her chin.

Gali finished her drink, tossed out her cup, and straightened her shoulders. This was it. She was going to be professional, but honest. She wasn't going to get too personal. She walked toward the door. She wasn't going to say anything about —

"It's about my husband," she burst out as she entered the supervisor's office.

Mrs. Rappaport looked at her steadily as Gali felt herself turn red. Where had that come from? So much for dignity...

"Why don't you sit down?" Mrs. Rappaport said kindly, indicating the worn armchair in front of her desk.

Gali sat, feeling shaken. She stared at the desk in front of her. The surface was littered with case files, notepads, and memos. There were picture frames with the Rappaport children on the side, and hanging on the wall were all of Mrs. Rappaport's degrees and awards. It was a welcoming room, but right at this moment, all Gali felt was nervous. She looked up and met Mrs. Rappaport's warm brown eyes.

"So tell me about your husband, Gali," the supervisor said.

Gali told her. She explained how Dovi was struggling, how he had made a new friend, a bad friend, a friend who was slowly preying on his doubts and insecurities and was pushing him further and further over the precipice. She told Mrs. Rappaport about how she'd had Avrami Meyers and his daughters for Shabbos and how Ora was now her client. And lastly, she told Mrs. Rappaport what Ora had told her about her father; what she, Gali, strongly suspected Mr. Meyers to be guilty of; how she could not tell Dovi this information; and how that was slowly but absolutely killing her.

She was a good listener, Mrs. Rappaport, her eyes following Gali's, her face mirroring the expressions on Gali's face, and she didn't interrupt even once.

Finally, Gali ran out of words. She leaned forward and plucked a tissue out of the box on the supervisor's desk. She wiped her face, and Mrs. Rappaport sighed.

"Gali, it must be so hard for you to deal with all of this."

Gali nodded, embarrassed at how good that validation made her feel.

"First of all," the supervisor said, "you were right in assuming that you cannot share the information about Mr. Meyers with your husband. It would be completely unethical and illegal, from both a lawful and halachic standpoint. I understand the position that puts you in, and I am sorry, truly. But Hashem is the one in charge, and if He wants Dovi to know, then he will, don't you worry."

Gali nodded soundlessly, disappointment flooding her. She had really been hoping for some sort of loophole, some leeway, where she would be able to share what she knew with Dovi.

"Secondly," Mrs. Rappaport continued, "I understand why you want to give Ora over to one of the other counselors, and I fully support your decision, although I'm worried about how she will cope with this change. She's had so many upheavals in her life... At her interview, she seemed rather...delicate. Frail, almost," the supervisor said, a touch sadly. "Poor girl, who knows the extent of what she has been through?"

Gali buried her face in her hands. It was true; switching social workers now could disrupt any progress Ora had been making. Her heart ached for Ora, who would now be bounced to another therapist. But considering the personal baggage Gali had involved here, there really wasn't any other choice...

Mrs. Rappaport gave a dry chuckle, and Gali looked up. The supervisor's eyes were soft and sympathetic. "It's a hard career we've chosen for ourselves, isn't it?" she asked rhetorically, and Gali nodded, her heart heavy. It *was* a hard career, full of choices and crossroads. But there was nothing like helping another person find her way in this world, and that was something she was actually good at doing, *baruch Hashem*. Though when it came to her own husband, it was a whole other story...

Gali thanked Mrs. Rappaport and stood up, her eyes lingering on the framed photos of her children.

"Gali."

She looked up, startled, and met Mrs. Rappaport's eyes once more.

"*Hatzlachah* with everything," the supervisor said softly.

Blushing, Gali thanked her and walked out. The dilemma was no longer in her hands. The fates of Ora Meyers, her father, and Dovi were now solely up to Hashem. Which they had been all along. Sometimes it just took a little perspective in order to see that, Gali realized.

She left the office and reached the bus stop just as the bus pulled up. Getting on, she went to the back and sat down, her heart slightly lighter as she headed home.

CHAPTER THIRTY-ONE

The door creaked open.

"Gali?" The whisper cut across the room.

Gali felt like her head was stuffed with newspapers — they'd only arrived at her parents' home a few hours ago, after a long and exhausting flight — but she managed to prop herself up on one elbow. "Shan?"

"Ahhh! You're really here!" Shani squealed softly, coming in and perching on the edge of Gali's bed. She gave Gali a big hug.

Gali closed her eyes and accepted the embrace; she had missed her little sister terribly.

"Go back to sleep," Shani said. "We'll schmooze later. Love you!"

"Love you, too," Gali croaked, and she was sleeping again by the time the door closed.

She awoke later to find the room dark, but she spied the sun's outline shining through the blinds. She glanced at her watch. It was a quarter past eleven. She yawned and pulled Yair's carriage toward her. It was empty. Dovi must have taken him out when he got up, so that she could sleep in. That was nice of him.

She threw on a robe and stumbled over suitcases into the hallway and down the stairs.

The sounds of voices and laughter were spilling out of the kitchen, and she made a beeline for it. She stopped, just short of the entranceway, and gazed at the scene with wide eyes. Yair was lying on a blanket in the corner of the room, drooling happily. Gali's mother was seasoning a pot of chicken soup, muttering to herself about shopping lists, while Shani and Chana, Gali's two sisters, chattered happily as they peeled their way through a mound of potatoes. Her brother Shlomo, married just over a year, had his head in the fridge and was shouting something about how his wife Layala really needed cottage cheese and could someone please help him find it.

Gali's eyes started burning. She still couldn't believe she was really here. This was her family, her beautiful, beloved family, and for once, it was *her* baby lying there in the thick of it all.

She walked into the kitchen and headed straight for her mother's arms.

"Gali!" her mother exclaimed. "You're finally up!"

Everyone started talking at once, about how cute Yair was and how excited they all were to see him and Gali and Dovi, but all Gali heard was the steady beat of her mother's heart as she hugged her tight. She inhaled the scents of vanilla and chicken soup that clung to her mother's robe.

"Mommy," she whispered, and the tears finally fell.

LATER THAT NIGHT, she stumbled into the kitchen for a cup of tea before heading to bed. Jetlag was hitting hard, and all she really wanted to do was sleep. Her mother was sitting at the table, keeping an eye on a pot on the stove as she murmured Tehillim from the *sefer* in front of her. Gali stared at the scene, so familiar from her childhood, and once more she felt the tears prick her eyelids.

Esther Lerner looked up, her eyes tired but happy. "My Gali," she said softly. "Are you alright, *bubbelah*?"

Gali swallowed hard. *No*, she wanted to say. *No, Mommy. I'm not alright. Hold me tight, hug me, please, make things all better, just like you used to...* But she said none of those things, because she knew that with all of her mother's love and good intentions, she could *not* make things all better for Gali now.

"I'm fine," Gali murmured. "Just tired, really. I thought a hot tea might be good before I go to sleep."

Her mother got up. "Let me make it for you." She shoved Gali gently into a chair. Gali sank into it like a stone.

"It's nice to be taken care of, for a change," she said, closing her eyes. She wanted to take advantage of this delicious moment, just her and her mother, and open up to Mommy about these past few turbulent months. But she was just so *tired*, so exhausted from holding everything together, all of the time... After just a few sips of her tea, she felt her eyelids close. Gali felt a warm arm around her, guiding her to the couch, and the sweet scent of vanilla floating by as she drifted off into dreamland.

ॐ

THE TWO DAYS LEADING UP TO PESACH were its usual mess of pizza parties in the backyard, last-minute shopping, and *sheitel* appointments, and then finally, it was time. The acrid smell of smoke filled the backyard as Gali's father burned the *chametz* in the barbeque grill. Her mother was already back inside, making *Pesach'dige lokshen*, and the grandchildren, who had gotten up way too early that morning, were being shepherded into their beds for naps. Gali looked around for Dovi and found him sitting on the glider, Yair lying on his lap, gently swinging back and forth.

She walked over, feeling supremely unnatural, and sat down next to him.

Dovi smiled at her in greeting, but then he sighed. "It's like a scene from a book," he said. "The characters are all so predictable: father burns the *chametz*, mother cooks, grandchildren play around. But how do I get back into the scene, Gali? I feel like I'm an outsider looking in, trying to understand. Except that I don't. I can't."

Gali was silent. She was tired of his angst. She was tired of his pessimism. Quite frankly, she was tired of the whole new Dovi, the person he had become lately.

She looked at him, at the crease between his eyes, at the defeated expression on his face, and suddenly, the pity that she had thought was long depleted filled her up once more.

"You'll get there, Dovs," she said softly. "You just need time. But for now, why not just enjoy? Let's play with Yair, eat way too much good food, and go on relaxing Chol Hamoed trips... There's no pressure here — just a bunch of loud family members who really love you."

Dovi cracked a smile.

"I'm going in to help my mother with the cooking. You okay with Yair?"

He nodded. "Yup, we're good."

She let out a sigh. "Great. See you soon," she said, and walked back toward the house.

Gazing darkly into the distance, Dovi did not even respond.

❧

"Switch magazines with me; I read this one already," Chana said, taking the one Gali had just picked up.

"No," Gali protested, pulling back and laughing.

"Shan-Shan?" Chana asked sweetly.

"Nope." Shani didn't even look up.

"Girls, you need to share," Mrs. Lerner joked, and they all started laughing.

Gali pretended to pout as she handed over her magazine to Chana, and Shani started to sing, "Gali did a mitzvah, a mitzvah, a mitzvah..."

Gali sighed with satisfaction. Living in Eretz Yisrael was an amazing opportunity, and she appreciated it anew every day, but that didn't mean she didn't miss her family back in America. True, Chana lived in Eretz Yisrael, too, and the two sisters tried to see each other as much as possible, but it wasn't the same as being back in the nest in Baltimore, back with Mommy and Ta and Shani and Shlomo and the rest of the crew. Oh, how she had missed the old three-story house she'd grown up in, with its creaky stairs, cushioned window seats, and the scent of fresh laundry wafting up from the basement. The porch they all sat on now overlooked a large backyard, lush with freshly mowed grass and trees wearing their new spring buds proudly.

She gazed at the swing set she'd played on as a child, with its rope swings, curved slides, and canvas roofs. She had long imagined her own children perched in various positions on its appendages. There'd be a little boy, perhaps two years old, with long, straight, golden-brown hair falling down his shoulders because he refused to allow her to tie it up. He would be on the tire swing, maybe leaning on his stomach, his little sandal-clad feet kicking up clouds of dirt every time he pushed off. Her daughter, maybe five, with thick, dark hair and Dovi's large blue eyes, would be sitting on another swing, pumping back and forth and calling out to Gali, "Look at me, Mommy! Look at me..."

She tore her eyes away from the swing set to find the porch quiet. Her sisters were looking at her, and was that pity in their eyes?

"I'm sorry, I spaced out there for a moment," she said briskly. "Must be jetlag still... So Shan, how's tenth grade treating you?"

The silence stretched while Gali silently begged them all to just let it go, just let it go... Because if they pried, she would relent from the pressure and swing open like an old gate, revealing all the ugliness and neglect of her once-happy life...

Thankfully, they did let it go. Shani finally grinned and began to relate a funny story about her G.O. head, Chana fell asleep over her cherished magazine, Layala came out and joined them, and Mrs. Lerner kept tearing up about having "all my girls together again." Gali sat back, taking it all in, silently thanking the others for allowing her the dignity to remain intact for just a little longer.

She knew she couldn't keep what was going on in her life completely from her family. By the time Yom Tov ended, her parents and siblings were bound to have picked up on something or other from the hardships she was facing. But for now she held onto her innermost feelings for just a little longer.

ॐ

"STRIKE!" GALI CALLED OUT, and a great explosion of back-slapping and high-fiving broke out as Dovi took an exaggerated bow. Gali lifted Yair in the air and held up his hand. "High-five me!" she squeaked, and laughing, Dovi gave the little hand a soft pat with his large one.

He was doing a great job at playing the "old Dovi," and no one in the family had said anything to indicate otherwise. Of course, there had been that awkward moment when Gali had walked into a room filled with her father, brother, and brother-in-law, and they had all stopped talking and turned red. So maybe they had noticed *something*. But Gali had no emotional energy to think into that at all. She just hoped they had more tact in front of Dovi himself.

Now they'd all gone bowling for a Chol Hamoed trip. Gali snickered, remembering the first time Dovi had gone bowling with her family. It was Chol Hamoed Sukkos, and they had recently gotten engaged. Dovi had come in to spend time with Gali and her family. Shani was just a few years old, and Shlomo, trying his hardest to impress his soon-to-be brother-in-law, had thrown his bowling ball a little too high. They'd all watched in horror as it ricocheted off the back wall, sending chunks of plaster flying and nearly striking down at least three people in the bowling alley.

Gali remembered her mortification, but mostly, she remembered how easygoing Dovi had been about the whole thing. He had just laughed and clapped Shlomo on the shoulder, and then he had gone to help clean up the mess. She'd watched him go, perhaps realizing for the first time the full extent of her *chassan's* shining *middos*.

They'd gone to his car after the game was over, waving to her family, and then they sank into the seats with exaggerated relief.

"Phew!" Gali had said.

"Yeah," Dovi had answered. They stared at each other and then burst out laughing.

"Kicked out of bowling alley!" Dovi howled. "Chunks of plaster! Little old lady nearly bowled over!"

Gali laughed and laughed along with him, until tears ran from her eyes. Every time she pictured Shlomo's shocked face, it set her off again, and every time she calmed down, she'd look at Dovi and then burst out laughing once more. And she remembered thinking, as they'd finally hiccupped to a comfortable silence, how lucky she was that she would be spending the rest of her life together with this wonderful, tall *yeshivah bachur* sitting next to her...

She blinked and brought herself back to the present. He was still tall, her husband. And he was still wonderful. But he was no *yeshivah bachur* anymore. He was a chef for B'tei'avon Catering. He participated in cooking classes, listened to the radio, and carried around an iPhone. He was, well, a stranger.

But right now, as he stood next to Shlomo and her father debating bowling techniques, she just wanted to accept him. It was so hard to always be angry and sad, to always be disappointed in her husband... For just a second, as she jiggled the baby on her hip, she wondered what it would be like to join Dovi. What would happen if she threw in the towel and also went down a few rungs in her *Yiddishkeit*? What if she started wearing shorter skirts and lower necklines? What if they blasted radio music in their home until neither of them could hear the silent screams of their souls anymore? What if they vacationed wildly and partied with abandon?

She shuddered at these thoughts. No. It wasn't her. She couldn't; she wouldn't. Did Dovi want that from her? Did he want her to be cooler, more jaded? Did it rub him the wrong way that she had no *emunah* questions of her own, had no desire to have a more secular lifestyle?

"Your turn, Gals," Shani said just then, interrupting Gali's thoughts. She took Yair out of Gali's hands.

"Thanks," Gali heard herself say, and she walked toward the lane, her mind still spinning.

Dovi grinned at her, but all she could do was stare unseeingly back at him as the thoughts whirled endlessly through her mind.

৵

"NEVER," HE SAID ADAMANTLY.

Gali lowered her eyes. She didn't want him to see how badly she wanted to believe that one word.

They had been sitting on the glider, watching the sunset, when Gali had broken down and told Dovi about her wild thoughts of the morning.

"Gali," he said quietly. "Gali, look at me."

She felt her eyes fill with tears. She was so afraid to hear what he would say, so afraid to gaze into his eyes and see his soul. But she looked at him steadily, and was shocked to find tears rolling down his cheeks, too.

"Gali," he choked, "you may not realize it, but you are my rock, my lifeboat. Your steadfastness, your unwavering faith in me, in Hashem

— those things are going to be the light that shows me the way home one day. Rabbi Gordon believes it will happen, and I...I trust him. But I need to know that you, the same you that I married, are what I am going to be coming home to. Because right now, we both know how lost I am, and everything is so cloudy, so hazy, so full of pain — but when I look at you, when I look at your strength and your purity, the smoke clears, and I can see straight again, if only for a minute." He stopped to catch his breath, the tears clogging his throat, making his voice thick and heavy.

"So don't change, Gali. Don't change because of me. Because I need you to stay as you are. I need it more than you can ever know."

And he placed his hands over his face and he cried as he'd never cried before. Gali joined him, and as the sun slowly set, painting the landscape in reds and pinks, the sounds of crickets and soft weeping were all they could hear.

CHAPTER THIRTY-TWO

The heart-to-heart with her mother never happened. Every time Gali found herself alone with her mother, she'd open her mouth — and then change the subject. She wasn't sure what it was that made her hold back, despite wanting so badly to confide in her mother. Did she not want to worry Mommy? Or was it her pride? Did she so cherish the image she upheld of having it together, of being stronger than her *nisayon*, of conquering and fighting and winning against all odds? Was that it? Did she not want her mother to know the truth? The truth was that she, Avigayil Lerner Rothman, was a loser. A big, helpless loser. She couldn't have a baby. She couldn't keep her husband from sliding in his *Yiddishkeit*. And she couldn't keep her foster son. Not a lot of *nachas* reports coming from her address...

She sighed and peeled the tape that read "*Chametz!*" off her mother's china cabinet. It had been a beautiful Yom Tov, and Gali couldn't believe how close she had come to missing out on it. So she hadn't allowed herself the luxury of unburdening her heart to her mother. Still, the time spent with her parents and siblings had fortified her, strengthened her for whatever storms still lay ahead.

But at this point, she wasn't even sure if strength would be enough. That's why she was praying for a miracle.

ঌ

HE TIPTOED OUT OF THE ROOM, squinting at the clock on his way out. It showed 2:23 a.m. He grabbed his flute case and closed the door behind him. The study light was off, and he didn't bother to turn it on. Leaning his head against the coolness of the window, he watched the lights of the city twinkle as he let his eyes glaze over. He was tired — they had landed back in Israel just a few hours ago — but he couldn't sleep, and he knew it wasn't only because of jetlag.

Was life always going to be this complicated? Would the pain of his anger, the sting of his frustrations, always be this strong? Or would it fade with time, until he was one of those men whose eyes look sad, yet steady?

Is that what he had to look forward to? A time when he would have accepted his disappointments instead of wallowing in them?

He gazed out at the streets of Jerusalem for a while longer, his breath fogging up the glass. He wiped the smudge off the window and noticed, with some sadness, that it disappeared, as if he had never been there. He felt the tears start as he backed away from the window.

Shutting the study door, he lifted his flute and began to play. Slow, mournful notes floated through the air as the hours slowly passed with him playing in the dark, trying vainly to turn all of his sorrow into song.

ﾞﾚ

SHE YAWNED SO WIDELY, she felt her jaw crack. Jetlag was once again striking her in full force, and it didn't help that the baby was completely off schedule; he had been up all night, wide awake and ready to play.

Gali roamed the aisles of the supermarket in slow motion, filling up her cart with milk, bread, and baby food. She also added a bag of flour. She hadn't done any serious *chametz* baking since they'd gotten back to Eretz Yisrael, and she was sure Dovi would appreciate a fresh batch of cinnamon buns. She was just reaching for a carton of eggs when she heard a familiar, high-pitched voice having a very loud conversation with an unknown party. Gali backed silently into the candy aisle, trying to place the voice. A small, thin woman came into view, and then it clicked: Aviva Brach's mother.

Gali held her breath. This was one of the worst parts of being a social worker. She *hated* meeting clients or their families out of the office. They always eyed her warily, as if waiting for her to spill their deepest and darkest secrets to the entire public world. *I have other interests in life besides your issues, you know!* she always wanted to say to them whenever this happened.

She really had no time for this now. Forgoing the eggs, she spun her cart around and ran to pay for her groceries before Mrs. Brach saw her.

Gali loaded her groceries into the bottom of Yair's carriage and headed home. She realized how impossible it would have been for her to continue as Ora Meyers's social worker. If she couldn't handle meeting a client's mother in the supermarket, how would she manage having a client who might pop by her house at any time with her father?

Gali was confident: she had made the right decision. Ora needed a new social worker, a new therapist. Now for the hard part...telling her.

ૐ

"But I don't understand!"

Gali flinched at the high-pitched screech. She stared at Ora. The normally placid, cool girl was a red-faced, hysterical mess. Gali threw Mrs. Rappaport a helpless look. The supervisor just shrugged her shoulders apologetically and left the room to go call Tikva Singer, the social worker who would be taking over for Gali. Gali realized she had around five minutes to make the transfer a smooth procedure.

"It's really going to be okay," she said soothingly, pushing a box of tissues across the desk.

Ora grabbed the entire box and held it firmly in her hands, as if scared that it, too, would leave her. "But I hate change," she whimpered.

Gali's heart broke. Of course she hated change! Her parents had gotten divorced, she had moved to Israel, she was battling her own body... *Nothing* in the girl's life had remained stagnant in who knew how long!

"I'm sorry, Ora," she said in what she hoped was a kind but firm tone. "I just feel that it wouldn't be professional for me to continue counseling you, because we are almost...friends." The words sounded lame, even to her own ears. Right, like a teenager was going to buy that.

But Ora sat up straighter at those words, and her face opened up slightly.

Gali sat back, startled. Huh? Who would have known... Feeling slightly encouraged, she continued in that vein. "As a social worker, it wouldn't be right for me to have you over for Shabbos, or to have you involved in my personal life, and I don't want to end all of that. But if you start seeing Mrs. Singer, instead of me, then we can keep on being friends. Do you see what I'm saying?" Her eyes searched Ora's hopefully.

Tikva Singer knocked just then and entered, a bright and professional smile on her face. Gali liked Tikva but found her to be a bit... much. She was too professional, in Gali's opinion, too much by the book, too proper...but she was a genuinely kind person, and Gali knew she was going to take good care of Ora.

Ora didn't seem to feel the same way. She took one look at Tikva and started crying again. "I can't start all over!" she wailed. "I won't! I'll leave this place! I'll go back to my father. And then whatever he does to me will be *your* fault!" She sobbed, dropping her head into her hands.

Gali stared wide-eyed at Tikva, who, for once, looked like she had no idea what to do next. The books didn't always prepare you for every situation...

"Ora," Gali said gently, standing up and walking around her desk until she was crouching at the girl's side. "Ora, what do you mean, 'whatever he does to me'? What does your father do to you, exactly?" She sucked in her breath, knowing that whatever Ora was about to say about her husband's close friend and business partner she would not be allowed to share with him.

Ora scrunched up her face and twisted a tissue between her thin fingers. She looked up, past Gali, at Tikva, who was standing there, an unreadable expression on her face.

"Never mind," she whispered. And she wouldn't say another word.

৶

THE OFFICE WAS EMPTY. Ora had gone to lie down, and Gali finally had a moment to stop and process the events of the past hour. Her thoughts were a jumble of professional rules and emotional opinions, but all of that was trumped by one huge, glaring need. She would go find Tikva and discuss it with her, but at the end of the day, she would make sure it was done: she was going to ensure that Avrami Meyers was reported to the Israel Association for Child Protection.

CHAPTER THIRTY-THREE

The phone rang, cutting through the dark. Immediately, Yair woke up and started shrieking.

Gali groaned. Who on earth calls someone at six thirty in the morning? Half-asleep, she stumbled out of bed toward the baby's room, just as Dovi's hand emerged from under his covers, groping around blindly for his ringing phone.

Gali picked up Yair and nuzzled him softly. His startled cries petered off into self-righteous moans, and finally, he fell back asleep. She rocked him a while longer, and then gently returned him to his crib.

Gali walked back to her room, still wondering who the caller was. She found Dovi staring out the window, one hand holding his phone away from his ear as a loud voice kept up a steady stream of angry yelling. She raised an eyebrow at him, but he just shook his head, rolled his eyes, and motioned for her to go back to sleep. She did, figuring she'd hear all about it at a more decent hour.

ॐ

DOVI WAS OUT by the time she woke up again. For one glorious second, she imagined he went to an early *minyan* and yeshivah, like he used to, but then reality hit. He was probably picking up coffee somewhere, or something of the sort. She sighed and went to wash her hands before putting up hot water.

She was just sitting down to a protein bar and a cup of brewed hazelnut when Dovi strolled in, carrying a pastry bag and an iced coffee.

She grinned. She knew him too well.

"Good morning," she said, smiling over the rim of her cup.

He sat down next to her and pulled out a chocolate croissant. "You want some?"

She smiled and shook her head. "I'm fine, thanks."

He shrugged, made a *brachah*, and bit in.

"So what is it?" she asked patiently.

He looked up. "What is what?" he responded innocently.

She rolled her eyes. "Come on. You only buy takeout breakfast when you're stressed. Now, out with it!"

Dovi laughed and took a sip of iced coffee. "Okay, okay, you got me," he said in mock defeat. "I just know you're not such a fan of Avrami Meyers..."

Gali gagged on her bar. "Avrami Meyers?" she choked. "What about him?"

Dovi sighed. "That early morning phone call was him, calling to vent. It seems somebody reported him to, get this, Child Protective

Services, or the Israeli equivalent of that. He's guessing it was his ex-wife. I mean, that's a pretty low thing to do, don't you think?"

Gali sat there silently, letting Dovi ramble on, until he finally caught on to the fact that she hadn't said a word. "Gals?" he said. "Everything okay?"

Gali swallowed hard. "Yeah," she said eloquently. "I mean, yes. Just, wow, that's really, uh, something. So what is he going to do?"

Dovi was still looking at her worriedly, but thankfully, he dropped it. "He doesn't know, really," he said. "He just called me blustering about how he doesn't need strangers poking into his life, and if they'd know what a good father he is, they'd be begging him to give parenting classes, etcetera, etcetera."

Gali almost choked, but she managed to keep a semi-blank face. "I see," she said. "Poor guy."

Dovi sighed. "I think I'll go over and cheer him u—"

"No!" Gali said loudly, and Dovi blinked.

"Why not?" he asked.

"Because I wanted to take Yair on a picnic. With you," she said hastily.

"Huh?" Dovi said. "Gali, you have work, remember?"

"I'm taking the day off," Gali said slowly, running through her schedule mentally to see if that was even possible.

"Oh," Dovi said. He was looking at her oddly, but all he did was drain his iced coffee and stretch. "Okay, well, I'm excited," he said brightly. "How about I whip us up some whole-wheat wraps with avocado egg salad and vinaigrette tomatoes?"

Gali smiled gratefully. "That sounds amazing," she said, standing up and trying to figure out where her day went. Once again, it was

Avrami Meyers's fault. She went to call Healthways. Apparently, she was taking a mental health day...

Ironic, wasn't it?

কৣ

SHE WAS HUMMING as she stood before the light pink door. The day off had been unplanned, but she had truly enjoyed herself. She couldn't remember the last time she had really spent time with Dovi for no specific reason other than to just enjoy his company. Which she had. She smiled and rapped lightly on the door.

"Come in," a clear voice called out.

Gali blinked and entered. She took in the neatly made bed, two zipped suitcases, and the girl wearing a handbag standing in front of her. For once, Gali was at a complete loss for words.

Aviva smiled. "I'm leaving," she said simply.

Gali stared at her. "How...? When...?" she stuttered.

"Yesterday," Aviva said, going over to grab her sweater out of the closet. "That's when Mrs. Rappaport gave me the green light."

Gali just stood there, feeling disoriented. "Yesterday," she repeated dumbly. Yesterday, while she was out picnicking with Dovi and Yair...

Aviva gave a light laugh. "Yeah. I think they just need you to sign a few papers, and then I am out of here."

Gali stared at her, remembering the emaciated, sick girl from so many months ago. That person bore no resemblance at all to the pretty, normal-looking — albeit thin — girl in front of her now.

"Wow," Gali said finally. "I-I'm really happy for you."

Aviva flushed. "Thank you."

Gali cleared her throat. "Well, I'd better go find those papers and do some signing," she said, turning to leave.

Aviva raised a hand. "Wait," she said, her voice faltering.

Gali turned to look at her, brown eyes meeting blue.

Aviva's voice was low. "Thank you...for everything. You saved me. You made me believe in change, believe in myself..."

Gali cut her off. "It has truly been a pleasure, Aviva," she said, feeling an inexplicable lump in her throat.

Aviva gave a small smile. "Well, goodbye then..."

Gali gazed at her. "Goodbye," she said, and turning, she closed the light pink door behind her with a click and a whispered prayer for the girl behind it.

ૐ

"How did this happen?" Gali barged into Mrs. Rappaport's office, waving Aviva's release papers in the air.

Mrs. Rappaport put down the coffee she had been sipping. "Hello to you, too, Gali," she said, eyes twinkling.

"You gave Aviva the go-ahead for this?!" Gali cut in. "To leave Healthways?!"

Mrs. Rappaport nodded. "Of course. I mentioned the idea to you a week or so ago, in the kitchen, remember?"

Gali searched her memory. She remembered sipping her coffee in brooding silence while Mrs. Rappaport chatted away to her at the table, but for the life of her, she couldn't remember what the supervisor had been saying. She had so much on her mind these days, was it any wonder she had trouble remembering a chance comment from her supervisor? Even if it was about a client as close to her heart as Aviva Brach?

Mrs. Rappaport was still talking. "Her weight is stable, she's at no risk to herself or others... *Baruch Hashem*, she's doing so much better. It's a wonderful thing, Gali."

Gali deflated, all the indignation she'd been carrying leaving her in one resigned swoop. It was all true. Aviva *was* doing so much better. Gali had just been too preoccupied to notice. *Social Worker of the Year, right here*, she thought sardonically.

"You're right," she said softly. "It *is* a wonderful thing. I'm really happy for her. I just...I wanted..." How could she explain that, awful as it sounded, she was afraid to let go of one more thing in her life? That this would now make Aviva into another constant that she would have to say goodbye to?

"I think she'll do fine, Gali," Mrs. Rappaport said, her voice gentle. "You really gave her the tools she needs to go out into the world and make something beautiful of herself."

Gali smiled gratefully at her supervisor's words. "I should go sign these papers, then," she said, backing quietly out of the office.

Mrs. Rappaport stared after Gali for a moment. Then she shook her head, and sighing a deep, sad sigh, went back to her papers.

CHAPTER THIRTY-FOUR

ou, me, and three hours of the world's finest musicians, including Jeffry Culliver, world-renowned flutist," Dovi said, flourishing the tickets grandly as Avrami pummeled dough for garlic bread. He missed good music; he regretted breaking his flute.

"Ungh," Avrami grunted.

Dovi smirked. "Great, it's settled then." He put the tickets back into his pocket and looked sideways at Avrami.

There was silence and then, "I'm not going to no concert with you," Avrami muttered.

"Hmm?" Dovi asked, trying to tie his apron. The string was knotted, and he struggled while Avrami watched him, forehead furrowed in annoyance.

"I'm not going to your ridiculous concert. When will you realize, Rothman, that the answers you're looking for can't be found in musical notes? Now if you want to forget about life for a night, I know people."

Dovi gave up on the knot and just let the strings hang down. "No thanks," he said. "Tell your *people* that they are missing out on some real good music."

Avrami punched the dough slightly harder than necessary. "Trust me, they don't care."

Dovi started chopping onions. "Bro, what happened with the Association of Child Protection?"

Avrami squinted. "None of your business," he growled.

Dovi shrugged. "Fine." He tipped the onion slices into a pot.

"They're ruining everything!" Avrami blurted out. "They're destroying my life!" He grabbed a knife, and for a moment he looked half-mad, his hair standing on end, his face bathed in sweat. But then he started slicing portobello mushrooms, and Dovi felt himself soften.

"I'm sorry," he said quietly. "My wife is a social worker, so I know how it can—" He stopped mid-sentence, because Avrami was suddenly an inch away from him.

"Your wife is a *what*?" Avrami asked, his voice dangerously low. His eyes glowed, and for a moment, Dovi was afraid.

He straightened his back, reached out a hand, and gently shoved Avrami a few feet back. "A social worker," he said evenly. "She works for Healthways Eating Disorders Clinic. I thought you knew that."

Avrami's breathing was coming out in short spurts, so that he sounded like a tea kettle. "It was her!" he rasped. "She told on me! She reported me! She ruined everything! It was *your* wife. *Your wife!*" he shouted.

Dovi stared at him, his eyes cold. "Meyers, don't talk about things you don't know," he said. "My wife doesn't care about your personal life. She has bigger things on her mind."

Avrami started pacing. "It all makes sense now!" he breathed. "Ora...the clinic she's at... And your wife..." He stopped suddenly and spun around to face Dovi. "You can call them off!" he said.

Dovi blinked, keeping his eyes on the knife in the other man's hand. "Call whom off?"

Avrami slammed his hand down on the counter, sending green peas flying. "The social workers!" he shouted. "Tell your wife to call them off. Tell her it's all a mistake."

Dovi stared at the man with whom he'd spent so much time this past year. He let his gaze roam over Avrami's bare head, down to his eyebrows, furrowed like two angry caterpillars. His eyes — windows to the soul, they say — were cold and empty, with an eerie fire dancing in their depths.

Dovi felt sick. "I need to go," he said, and just like that, apron and all, he turned and walked out the door. Avrami was so surprised, he didn't even try to stop him.

Which was a good thing, Dovi mused, as he jogged up the street and flagged down a nearby cab. Because he suddenly had the overwhelming desire to punch the living daylights out of someone.

ॐ

HE GOT OUT at the corner near his home. Walking past his building, he strolled to the park. The sun was beating down mercilessly overhead, and the neighborhood children were confined indoors until their mothers agreed it was cool enough to go out and play. But the heat didn't bother him. He sat on a metal bench, enjoying the warmth, his face tilted to the sun. Eyes closed, he saw spots in the darkness, bright splashes of colors he couldn't name.

So Gali had reported Avrami Meyers to the Israel Association of Child Protection. He mulled this over, waiting to feel anger or betrayal at his wife's actions toward his best friend, but all he felt was acceptance. If he knew anything for certain these days, it was that his wife was a genuinely good person. And she would never get another person in trouble with the law out of spite, for a personal vendetta. If she had indeed tipped the authorities off, it was because she knew something, something confidential, something bad.

He opened his eyes and sat up. It must have been so hard for Gali not to tell him, to watch him go off every day with a man she knew was a criminal, and just trust that he would come back to her later. His heart overflowed with gratitude. She was so special, Gali, so altruistic... And because of that, because of his wife's good heart, he sat on the park bench, the sun burning into his tiny suede yarmulke, and he did something he hadn't done in months. He opened his mouth and spoke to Hashem.

"Thank You for my wife," Dovi murmured, his eyes brimming. "Thank You for Gali." And then he got to his feet and slowly walked out of the deserted playground.

He decided not to tell Gali that he knew. It would just cause her angst over whether or not she could discuss the case with him, and she had enough on her plate these days. Shoshana would be coming to take Yair away in just a few short weeks, and Gali seemed to be running on autopilot, her hands and feet moving, but her gaze far, far away. He knew what she was trying to see. She wanted to see the future, to glimpse their days ahead, to see the colors they would be painted. Would the moments lob together in grays and browns, or would bursts of yellow and blue fill the cracks that Yair would leave behind?

"I'll be there for you!" Dovi wanted to shout. "You won't be alone! We're in this together!" But he refused to make promises he couldn't keep, and so instead he said nothing and just watched his lovely, vivacious wife turn into a fragile shell.

Avrami hadn't bothered trying to reach him; he knew Dovi well enough to understand that Dovi would never pick him over his wife, and so, it seemed, he wasn't going to push for Dovi's help. A couple hours after Dovi stormed out on Avrami, Dovi received just one short text from him: *Hired waiters for dinner.* That was all.

Was this Avrami's way of spurning their friendship? If so, Dovi was somewhat glad. He didn't want to cause Gali any unnecessary stress, and he knew that the less he hung out with Meyers, the better it would be for her. He and Avrami would do the dinner together — this was a professional job, after all — and then, Dovi decided, he would reassess. Was he ready to call it quits on their friendship completely, and on this catering job that he so much enjoyed? He wasn't sure. But he did know that things couldn't continue as they stood now.

And if he wanted to be really honest with himself, he was pretty sure that the Israel Association of Child Protection was going to find exactly what they were looking for when checking into Avrami. If anyone had guilt written all over him, it was Avrami Meyers and his knife-waving self.

CHAPTER THIRTY-FIVE

He moved from table to table, squirting dressing onto each salad plate. The dinner was starting in less than an hour, and only one waiter had shown up. He sighed and squeezed the bottle a little too hard.

"That's just great," he muttered as the plate of salad was drowned in dressing. He picked up the plate and went to switch it with an extra one from the kitchen.

On his way, he walked by the program room where seats and a podium had been set up. He was annoyed, plain and simple. Avrami was late, the waiters — hired by Avrami — were late, and once again, Dovi was the one working al—

"Whoops!" he exclaimed, moving aside just in time as a man with a black hat and red beard almost crashed into him.

"I am so sorry!" the man said, bending to pick up the soggy salad that had fallen off the plate.

Dovi sighed. "Don't worry about it," he said, bending to scoop it up himself.

The man got to his feet, knees creaking. "You must be one of the chefs. I met Mr. Meyers on a different occasion, so I'm guessing you're Mr. Rothman." He stuck out his hand to Dovi.

Dovi shook the man's hand with his lettuce-free one. "Guilty," he said, already turning to continue to the kitchen.

But the man held him back. "I'm Refael Litkowitz," he said, and Dovi was taken aback.

"*You* are Rabbi Litkowitz, keynote speaker for the convention tonight?" he asked incredulously. The man couldn't have been more than five years older than him.

The rabbi smiled. "Guilty," he said, and Dovi grinned. "I hope you have time to listen to the program tonight, Reb—?"

"Dovi."

"Reb Dovi," the rabbi said, letting go of his hand.

"I'll try," Dovi found himself promising.

The young rabbi smiled. "I'm glad." And with one last apology about the salad mess, he entered the program room, leaving Dovi even more off-schedule and even more confused.

Why had he said he'd listen to the program? He hadn't heard a *shiur* or a speech in months! But he couldn't help it. Inexplicably, he liked Rabbi Litkowitz. Anyway, what harm could listening to one speech do?

CHOCOLATE DRIPPED COPIOUSLY onto the table, creating splashed designs against the light wood. Dovi popped the apple slice into his mouth, licking chocolate off of his lips sheepishly. "Is it wrong that I want to dip my salad in here also?" he asked Gali, eyeing the pot of melted chocolate.

Gali giggled. "Please don't," she said. "You've already dipped the fruit, waffles, and even the breadsticks... I honestly don't know how it's not making you sick." She delicately dipped a waffle strip into the pot.

Dovi sighed happily. "Ah, if only I could dip everything in life into chocolate. My problems, my stress, my job..."

Gali giggled. "My doctors' appointments, my clients, Yair's mother..."

Now they were both laughing. "Avrami Meyers!" they said at the same time, and cracked up. They sat there laughing, while Yair gurgled happily in his highchair.

Gali calmed down first. "It's not a bad idea," she said, wiping her eyes. "It can be a new therapy: sweeten any problem in seconds!" She handed Yair a cracker to gnaw on.

Dovi chortled and took a sip of his milkshake. "We'll make a killing!" He raised his eyebrows in mock excitement.

Gali gave a half-smile. "That's one thing we don't need," she said quietly. "Although my doctor's appointment next week will cost a pretty penny..."

Dovi dropped his eyes. "Mmm-hmm," he acquiesced, and Gali's heart went out to him. Dovi had stopped getting excited about her doctors' appointments around seven years ago. Not that she could blame him; they hadn't offered her any hope in over five... But Dr. Manetti had sounded promising, and Gali couldn't help but continue dreaming. She reached out and tickled Yair's foot, purposely not meeting Dovi's eyes.

"Well, if it's *bashert* for something to come of the appointment, it will happen," he said seriously, and Gali almost fell off of her chair in shock.

"Um, excuse me?" she said, cocking her head to one side. Since when did the new Dovi say things like "*bashert*"?

Dovi shrugged and popped a grape into his mouth.

"Okay, now I know something's going on," she said, pointing at the grape. "You forgot to dip it in chocolate!"

He gave a small smile. "You ever heard of Rabbi Refael Litkowitz?" he asked her, dipping a spoon into the fondue and dragging it around in swirls.

"Of course!" Gali exclaimed. "I listen to his *shiurim* on the bus. He's an incredible speaker!"

Dovi nodded. "I know," he said. "Well, he was the keynote speaker last night, and I bumped into him... Long story short, he was speaking about *emunah*...and I don't know, suddenly, so many things made sense! So I went over to him afterward, and we ended up talking for over an hour...and I don't know, Gals, I feel...good." He spoke with his eyes cast downward, as if he was embarrassed about his feelings.

Gali felt tears enter her eyes, pricking her eyelids, filling her heart. "Thank You, Hashem," she whispered silently, her very soul singing with relief. Because now she knew. Now she knew that her jeans-clad, iPhone-toting, small-suede-yarmulke-sporting husband wasn't too far gone that he couldn't be reached. Now she knew that one day, no matter if it took months or years, her Dovi would return. And maybe that was her miracle.

She swallowed and tried to keep her voice even. "That's so nice," she said casually. "So are you keeping in touch?"

Dovi grinned at her exaggerated nonchalance. "We made a *chavrusa-shaft*," he said in the same tone, and Gali knocked over her chocolate milk.

"Sorry!" she exclaimed as Dovi jumped back from the table. But he was laughing.

"Well, that was more the kind of response I was expecting," he said, getting some paper towels and wiping up the mess.

Gali was so overwhelmed that she didn't even help him. She just sat there playing with Yair's chubby fingers. "So...what now?" she finally asked, her voice soft.

Dovi sat back down and looked at her. "Now we're patient," he said, just as softly. The two of them looked at each other, and twelve-plus years of understanding was apparent in their gaze.

"Okay," Gali answered, and she reached for a tomato from her salad. "Should I do it?" she asked him, indicating the pot of melted chocolate.

"Do it," he said.

So she dipped the tomato in chocolate.

It was pretty gross.

Chapter Thirty-Six

If a speeding train would come rushing at her right then, she didn't think she would be able to move aside. She sat, limbs frozen, eyes staring straight ahead, as something inside of her slowly died. She now wished Dovi had accompanied her because the task of repeating the day's events to him suddenly seemed harder than anything she had ever done before. She heard the clock tick; she would have to go pick up Yair from the babysitter soon. She thought of his toothy smile, of his little dimpled hands and small chubby feet, and she waited to feel something, anything. But she was numb, cold, and even more than that: she was finished. She was done with being strong, done with hoping. Because this whole time, while she had been doing all that, she had always believed that there was a stop somewhere along the way, and eventually, one day, she would get off this terrible vehicle called childlessness and arrive at that long-awaited station of mother-hood. But apparently, this ride was going nowhere.

Her eyes glazed over, and she just continued to stare at the wall opposite her until she heard the key turn in the lock.

"Gals?" Dovi asked, his voice anxious. He entered the room and just stopped. "What'd the doctor say?" he asked softly.

Gali looked up at him. He was wearing a black velvet yarmulke, regular-sized. She noticed this as if from far away, like she was looking through the wrong end of a telescope. Dovi had not worn a yarmulke like that in ages. Something inside her stirred at this. His *chavrusa-shaft* with Rabbi Litkowitz had been going really well. But that was probably all about to change now, wasn't it?

She thought of her husband's frail faith for a moment and won-dered if she would be wrong for sharing her news. But her pain was his pain, and she couldn't not tell him... She should really say goodbye to that black velvet yarmulke...

"Gali!" Fear made his voice sharper than usual, and she jumped. "Tell me!" Dovi said, coming to sit next to her.

She looked at him, at the husband she cared more about than herself, and the dam broke. She sobbed and sobbed, her entire body wracked with a pain too great for her to bear, and when she was all cried out, she cried some more. Dovi sat there, and he cried, too, for he understood what she was saying, but still, she needed to say it out loud.

"She told me...to stop trying." She swiped at her eyes. "This is the end of the line, Dovi. Hashem can perform *nissim*, of course He can, but...but He doesn't always decide to do them, does He?" She waited for his newfound faith to crumble, and sure enough, he rose to his feet and left the room.

She sat there, wondering how far she'd have to break before it would be impossible to piece her back together, when he returned, holding a tall glass of juice. "Drink this," he ordered softly, and only once he said that did she realize how thirsty she really was. She made a *brachah* and drank until the glass was finished.

"Can you pick up Yair?" she asked him, her voice trembling. "I think...I think I need to rest."

He adjusted the yarmulke on his head. "Of course," he said. "Gali, I'll do anything you need." There was some sort of promise in his words, it seemed, but she was too worn out to figure it out.

"Thank you," she murmured, and she stumbled off to her bed. Dovi sat there for a moment, embracing the pain for a little bit longer, before rising to his feet. It was time to get Yair.

❧

THEY SPENT A LOT OF TIME TOGETHER over the next few days, just the three of them, creating a bubble of sadness mixed with comfort that no one else could penetrate. They ate out, went on picnics, took Yair to the zoo and boardwalk, and visited parks. All the while, Dovi treated Gali as if she were fragile china, and she treated him warily, as if waiting for his yarmulke to come flying off.

Yair would be going home soon, and when he did, the golden glow of their home would be dimmed once more into what Gali knew would be a dark, cold, and all-consuming gray. But one positive thing that did penetrate into the dismal mist enveloping her was the fact that the more time Dovi spent with her and Yair and Rabbi Litkowitz, the less time he was spending with Avrami Meyers.

One more phone call clinched it. She had just entered the kitchen, hoping something would spike her appetite. She hadn't been hungry in days, and her already thin frame was starting to resemble those of some of her clients. She forced herself to eat square meals, but whatever she managed to choke down may as well have been sawdust.

Dovi had just hung up the phone and was shaking his head in disgust.

"What?" she asked him.

"It's Avrami..." Dovi said, forehead furrowed. "Has he always been this...arrogant?"

Gali hid a smile and turned away, choosing not to allow Avrami Meyers to drag her into the pitfalls of *lashon hora*. But inside, she was cheering.

Yes! she wanted to scream. *Avrami Meyers has always been this way. He is also a child abuser and a crook! Stay away from him, Dovi!* But all she said was, "Hmm? Dovi, what do you think about taking Yair to that kiddie play station in the mall?"

After that, something changed. Gali heard a lot less about Avrami Meyers over the next few days. And when she tentatively asked Dovi if he wanted to invite Avrami for a Shabbos *seudah* — just to see what he'd say — his face darkened, and this time, he was the one to change the topic.

That was the silver lining Gali had been looking for.

CHAPTER THIRTY-SEVEN

She neatly folded the pile of undershirts on her bed, hands moving mechanically. Tuck, tuck, fold. Tuck, tuck, fold. She worked until there was only one left. Then she picked it up.

"Look how teeny-weeny," she murmured, remembering the novelty of bringing home something so small. She buried her face in the sky-blue onesie, breathing in the scent of baby detergent and dreams. How did she get here? She used to be confident, positive, so sure of life and where it would take her...and now here she was, unable to pull her face out of a baby's undershirt.

She sighed and straightened up. Shoshana would be coming soon, and she still needed to finish packing the baby's clothes and give him a bath. She went to call Dovi to ask him to bring Yair to her, but first, she slipped the little blue onesie into the drawer in her nightstand.

She would keep it. For posterity. And for herself.

She lowered the baby gently into the bath, Dovi hovering at her shoulder. Yair gurgled and splashed his little feet. Gali blinked as water went into her eyes. She shampooed the baby's dark hair into soapy spikes, and when she couldn't help it anymore, the tears fell, splashing into the tub and rippling into nothingness. She sponged him off lovingly, marveling at how a baby that was of no blood relation to her at all could feel so completely a part of her soul.

She tried not to think about "lasts," but she couldn't help it. The last time she'd be giving Yair a bath. The last time she would diaper and dress him. The last time she would swaddle him and hold him close while he drank his bottle...

She felt the lump in her throat grow bigger, until it was so large she thought it would engulf her entire being. Eventually, there was nothing to do except sit and hold the baby and watch the minutes on the clock go galloping by in great, bounding leaps, and before she knew it, the doorbell was ringing.

She looked at Dovi. "I can't," she said, almost pleading.

He looked at her, and her own pain was mirrored in his eyes. "I'll answer it," he said, as if by doing that one task, he would be able to remove the burden of pain she carried.

She sat there and waited, until there she was: Yair's real mother, with the same green eyes. Shoshana looked good, though still slightly ragged and worn. She also looked as if she would rather be anywhere but there right then.

"Hi, Gali," she said, her voice almost harsh with pity.

Gali tried to smile. "Here you go," she said, holding out her arms. Her hands were shaking so badly, she was scared Yair would fall.

Shoshana blinked at this abrupt gesture, but she took him.

"Wait," Gali said. She scooped Yair back and squeezed him against herself. She kissed his smooth forehead, tears falling thick and fast down her face. "I love you," she choked, and Shoshana looked away.

Then Dovi came and took Yair. He walked around the room with him once, whispering something to him, and then he circled back. He kissed the baby and turned to Shoshana. "Thank you," he said, nodding at her.

Gali tried to say something gracious and appreciative, but all that came out was a sob, and so she just nodded through her tears until they left. Then she ran to her room and cried as her heart shattered into one thousand little pieces.

حꙅ

It was three days later that she laughed again. Dovi had been regaling her with the story of the bar mitzvah he catered the night before, and when he started imitating the four grandmothers, she laughed. They both stopped, startled at the sound.

Dovi gave a small smile. "I guess life goes on," he said, and Gali had to agree. As much as she wanted to curl into a ball and scream that life was unfair, the rest of the world was continuing — and she really had no choice but to join along.

She even hummed a little as she went to turn on her computer to check her emails that night. She scrolled down the list of emails in her inbox: Mommy...an online sale somewhere...a *tzedakah* request... Aviva Brach? What could Aviva have to say? Curious, she clicked on the email and leaned forward to read:

Dear Mrs. Rothman,

How are you? How's Healthways? I can't believe I'm writing this, but I actually kind of miss it!

Life's going really well, thank G-d. I've started working for an organization that assists under-privileged teens and young adults. I'm actually helping people, and it's the craziest feeling!

I still attend therapy, of course, but now I am able to open up to my mother, communicate better with her, and suddenly, everything seems easier.

I really just wanted to say thank you again. You changed my life. Your encouragement to change my perspective, to look at the glass as full as I want it to be, has set me on the path I am on now, and I can't thank you enough.

I hope everything works out for you and that Hashem repays you for all the good you do.

All the best,

Aviva

Gali leaned back and smiled, a bittersweet expression that reminded her how rusty her smile muscles were. It was a nice letter, and she appreciated it.

She turned off her computer and decided to go for a walk. Maybe she could take her own advice and figure out how to view the glass differently. Because right then, it was feeling pretty empty.

CHAPTER THIRTY-EIGHT

She sat up straight in bed. Was Yair crying? She washed her hands and was halfway to his room when she remembered that, no, Yair was not crying. Not in her home, anyway. And from the way things were going, it didn't seem that there would ever be another baby crying in that room again. She waited for the stab of pain that usually accompanied thoughts such as these, but it didn't come. Maybe it was just too late at night, maybe she was too tired, or maybe — and this was the worst possibility of all — she had simply come to terms with the situation.

She thought about going back to bed, but sleep held little escape for her; her dreams revolved around disappearing babies and cold, sterile doctors' rooms.

She padded downstairs, flicked on the lights, and popped a decaf capsule into her Nespresso machine. Then she grabbed the couch blanket, draped it around her shoulders, and went to add milk to her coffee. The warm liquid filled her insides, drawing heat to her freezing heart. Her work beckoned, overdue paperwork begging to be attended to — if she couldn't sleep, she might as well get something done — but why work when you can procrastinate; so she checked her emails first.

The first one was from Aviva, sent only two hours ago and marked, "Urgent!" A feeling of dread flooded her, taking the place of the warm coffee. What on earth was Aviva doing up at two o'clock in the morning? Hesitantly, she clicked on the email.

Dear Mrs. Rothman,

It's been a crazy night. Working for this organization has taken more out of me than I ever even knew I had, but in a good way. Instead of it being all about me and my feelings, it's all about helping others and making their lives better. Kind of the way you helped me. Minus the weigh-ins, of course. ☺

But tonight things just went crazy. A girl — maybe twenty years old — came in, bruised and hallucinating. We don't know her story, or where she came from, but the staff made sure she quickly received a hot shower, a good meal, and a bed for the night. She won't speak, but one thing she did do was ensure we took her baby. Yes, that's right. She had a baby girl with her. My supervisor is doing research, finding out whose it is, if it's hers legally, and what we should do with the little girl. But my supervisor told me this has happened before — and that we have an opportunity to place the baby in a home before the officials get involved.

If it turns out to be up to us, I immediately thought of you. The baby looks to be around four months old, and she's gorgeous, with big, blue eyes and a completely bald head.

The baby might not be hers, even; we really don't know. But I was so excited, I just had to write to you about it. Please let me know what you think.

All the best,

Aviva

ॐ

DAYS PASSED, and the sun was still rising and setting, much to Gali's surprise. Yair's absence seemed to fill every room, every nook, cranny, seat, and stair. She was so engulfed in missing him that when the rest of the world didn't feel the same pain as her, she was inexplicably hurt and shocked.

But she was just as surprised at herself for moving on with life. It wasn't what she expected. The dark clouds she'd assumed would hover in the absence of his presence were nonexistent. Instead, the months of fostering Yair had faded into one of those perfect memories, like her camp years or her wedding day. She and Dovi would sink into the couch with the camera and flick through pictures of him, laughing and reminiscing about his antics and sweetness.

But then Dovi would go to work or to Rabbi Litkowitz's, and Gali would be home alone, and then suddenly Aviva's email would pop into her mind: *The baby looks to be around four months old...big, blue eyes...*

She wanted that baby. She wanted her so badly, it was an almost physical pain. But she knew the code of ethics backward and forward, and she was pretty sure that accepting a baby from a former client was pushing the boundaries of inappropriate acceptance. She didn't even tell Dovi about the offer; she didn't want anything to distract him from his path of return. Her diagnosis from the doctor had pushed him to the very edge, but he was still hanging on by his fingertips. Still, she knew that even the slightest gust of doubt could cause him to go tumbling back down. And this time, who knew if he would ever be able to find his way up again?

•

SHE WANDERED THROUGH THE PARK behind her house, secure in the knowledge that now, at seven thirty in the evening, it would be empty. She pictured for a moment what other women were doing at this time of day. Images of Yair giggling in the bath, Yair cozy in fleece pajamas, and Yair slurping sleepily from a bottle filled her mind. It was bedtime, and other women were mothers, and so they were busy with their families at this time. But not Gali. No, she had the freedom to wander around the park alone, no strings attached, no responsibilities...no purpose. She felt aimless, just floating from day to day...

Aviva had sent another email. The baby's name was Rut, and she had no home. Gali had read that, and she knew that baby had to be hers. But it wasn't ethical; it wasn't right. She couldn't have a former client pull strings for her like that.

She sank onto a bench and tilted her head back to see the sky. Somewhere out there, a blue-eyed baby named Rut needed a mother. And here she was, needing a baby.

Sometimes she really hated her job.

Chapter Thirty-Nine

The waves crashed against the sand with a ferocious intensity, spraying them with salt and grit. Gali laughed and blinked water out of her eyes. Dovi opened his arms wide and embraced the waves, eyes shut tight and head held high. Gali watched him, one hand holding her kerchief firmly in place.

They'd gone on the boat ride for a little getaway of sorts, but the pain had made its way through the sand and spray, straight into her heart. It seemed there was nothing she could do to escape it, even temporarily.

Dovi went to return their life jackets, but she turned her back on the sea and walked away from the marina toward a long patch of sand. She kicked off her shoes, sat down, and stared at the pristine sky for one moment before closing her eyes.

An image rose swiftly, unbidden. Aviva had sent it to her just yesterday. A peacefully sleeping baby, as perfect and pristine as a china doll, with the attached message: *Baby Rut still needs a home!* She opened her eyes and dug her hands into the sand. She grasped the grains tightly before letting them slip between her fingers. *I still need a baby*, she thought, and suddenly, she was angry.

She looked up. Dovi was approaching. He spotted her, did a cartwheel, and fell over, getting sand all over himself. She couldn't help it; she laughed.

He shook the sand out of his hair and placed his yarmulke back on his head. "Why're you here?" he asked. He just meant alone on the sand, but she answered him seriously.

"I don't know," she said, and it was the truth. "Why *am* I here, Dovi?" she asked plaintively, and all pretenses fell away. All of her fun-loving nature and busy, fulfilling schedule suddenly meant nothing, and she was left with an aching emptiness inside of her.

Dovi looked at her. "Is 'for me' enough of an answer?" he asked, and he was serious, but it wasn't enough for her, at least not right now. She smiled sadly and turned her head to watch two siblings, perhaps children of one of the fishermen, roaming the boardwalk, building a sand castle. They were digging and digging, trying to create a moat, but the sand kept slipping into the hole. She wanted to shout out, to tell them that what they were doing was futile, that they should stop trying so hard, but she held back.

Instead, she said to Dovi, "There's a baby." He gave her a questioning look, not understanding, so she explained. "My client, my ex-client, has access to an unwanted baby. A young mother gave her up..."

Dovi stared at her.

"Can you imagine?" Gali whispered, mostly to herself. "Giving up a baby..." The kids in the sand were growing frustrated, and Gali watched as they tried using large rocks to keep the sand back. "I can have her, if I want," she went on. "But...it's not ethical. I can have my license revoked...or worse. Do I care, though?" She turned to Dovi, wanting an answer.

"Yes," Dovi said quietly. "You do."

He was right; of course he was. Helping people was in her very being; she needed to do it, she *had* to do it.

"And there are other babies in the world besides this one," Dovi continued, his voice still soft. "Both born and as-yet unborn. If Hashem wants us to have a baby, Gali, we will, somehow or other...but in a straight way."

Gali's eyes filled, and once again she felt like she was in a dream. Was this really *Dovi* giving her a boost in *bitachon*?

She got up and wandered over to the kids. "Wet the sand," she said to them in Hebrew. "It'll stay that way." They blinked at her, but she looked so non-threatening that they just followed her directive.

Satisfied, she turned and walked back toward Dovi. "Let's go home already!" she said, and Dovi grinned.

ﻉ

SHE WINCED AT THE SUNBURN on her lower arms and cheekbones. She felt overheated and uncomfortable, but it had been worth it. There was nothing quite like being out on the sea; it was rejuvenating.

She was applying aloe vera when someone rang the doorbell. Dovi was in the shower, so she ran to get it. It was Avrami Meyers.

"Is Dovi here?" he asked brusquely, gazing wildly over her shoulder.

Gali was frightened, but she didn't let it show. "He's unavailable right now," she said firmly, silently begging him to leave.

"I'll wait, then," he said, trying to push open the door.

"I'd prefer if you leave," she said, her voice trembling. Avrami stared at her, his eyes jumping like a madman's, and then he turned and marched away, slamming the door behind him.

She didn't tell Dovi what happened, but she didn't need to. They were sitting on the couch, eating brownies, when Dovi's phone pinged.

"Avrami has been arrested," he said wonderingly, looking up from the screen.

Gali blinked. "He has?" she asked hesitantly.

"Yeah... He wants my help with bail..."

"No!" Gali said loudly.

Dovi met her gaze. "Of course not, Gali. I want nothing to do with that man anymore." His voice was firm, as if there was not even a question in his mind about it.

She stared at him, so relieved she almost cried. "Oh, thank You, Hashem, thank You, Hashem," she said, and before accidentally saying too much, she quickly popped another brownie into her mouth.

🙐

Dear Aviva,

Thank you so much for thinking of me, but it would be unethical for me to accept any help or benefits from you, as you were once my client.

I do appreciate your thinking of me. It was very kind.

Hatzlachah with everything. It sounds like you are doing so well.

Keep up the good work,

Mrs. Rothman

P.S. Please make sure the baby finds a loving home...

CHAPTER FORTY

She believed in new beginnings. She believed in the spring during the cold snow, and the sun during the relentless rain. She believed in second chances and change; she was hopelessly naive in that way. Perhaps that was why it was so hard for her to accept the verdict of "never" when it came to having a child; she was just too much of a believer in the impossible.

"It's one of the amazing things about you," Dovi said through a mouthful of scrambled eggs.

She gave him a half-smile and took another sip of coffee.

"No, I'm serious," he said, wiping his hands on a napkin and reaching for another piece of toast. "I mean, anyone else would laugh if their husband wanted to return to yeshivah for half a day after leaving in such a manner. But you woke up early, made me a fancy breakfast, wrote me a note, and most exciting, made me fresh chocolate-chunk cookies to eat during the day and make all the other guys jealous."

Gali laughed, but she was blushing. "I've never stopped believing in you, Dovi. I nearly gave up hope sometimes, I was sad, I was disappointed — but I always knew you'd find your way back." They both blinked back tears and then laughed ruefully.

"We're just a bunch of emotions waiting to burst," Dovi joked, wiping his eyes. "Oh, Gals, before I forget, this is for you." He reached behind his chair and brought out a large, brown paper shopping bag. "Do with it as you wish," he said quietly.

She glanced inside. It held a tiny box and a bundle of clothing. She pulled out the box and opened it to reveal a glistening band of diamonds.

She gasped. "Dovi!" Her hand fluttered to cover her open mouth.

"It's called an eternity band," he said softly. "If you stuck with me during these stormy past few months, then I know we'll stick together forever, no matter what the future holds."

Gali was crying in earnest now. Dovi donned his black hat, so neglected of late, and *bentched*. Then he got up. "Have a great day, Gals," he said, giving her a little wave. "Oh, and the other stuff you can just throw out. Or burn. Whatever you like." A minute later he was gone.

Gali sat for a moment, staring at the ring, before sliding it onto her finger. It was a perfect fit. Dovi knew her ring size, of course.

The stones on it shone like a captured sun. It was extravagant, certainly, but between her and the kitchen, she had to admit she deserved it. She laughed a little at her self-righteousness and then got up to clear away the plates.

Suddenly, she remembered the bag. She picked it up and shook the rest of its contents out onto the table. Something fell and clattered to the floor. She bent to pick it up, a triumphant smile breaking out across her face. It was Dovi's iPhone. Then she looked at the clothing she held in her hands. They were two pairs of blue jeans.

ॐ

SHE STOPPED AT THE GARBAGE DUMPSTER on her way to the bus stop. She stared at it for a moment, eyes glazed as she thought about what the bag of clothing hanging off of her wrist represented. Dovi's changes had been so much more than skin deep, but it was the differences in his outer appearance that had stared her in the face, day in and day out, keeping the pain at the forefront of her mind all the time. The jeans, the tiny yarmulke, the obnoxious iPhone — she saw them as icons symbolizing these past torturous few months, during which her best friend of twelve years had turned into a virtual stranger. And now she was going to throw these icons away, with a *tefillah* on her lips that her husband remain on the true Torah path from here on...

She arrived at Healthways a tad early, but she didn't mind. Better early than late, after all. She couldn't stop smiling as she made her way toward her office. Her ring kept catching the light, and she felt like a new bride as she found herself examining her hand with excitement.

She was humming as she finished up some paperwork when someone knocked on her door. "Come in," she called cheerily, scrawling a signature at the bottom of a form.

"Um, Mrs. Rothman?"

Gali looked up to find Ora Meyers standing there. "Ora!" she gasped, so startled that she actually rose to her feet. "Ora, what are you doing here?"

The girl shifted from foot to foot uncertainly. "Um...I just saw you sitting here alone, and I guess I just wanted to tell you that I'm... I'm glad you gave my case over to Mrs. Singer... I mean, I'm sure you would have been great, too, but Mrs. Singer has put some wheels into motion that I've been waiting for, for a long time..."

Gali stared at the poor girl, trying to imagine the irreparable damage Avrami had wrecked upon his daughter to the extent that she was glad he was in prison. But all she said out loud was, "I'm so happy, Ora. We don't always know why Hashem does things, but sometimes we get a glimpse at the truth... Good luck with everything." She smiled warmly, sitting back down and picking up her pen once more.

Ora smiled back shyly, and Gali noticed how much healthier she looked. "Thanks, Mrs. Rothman," she said, and then she quietly left.

Gali waited until the door closed, and then she put down her pen again and said a *perek* of Tehillim for the continued *hatzlachah* of Ora Meyers.

CHAPTER FORTY-ONE

The sound of one hundred voices arguing loudly was the first thing he heard as he stepped into the familiar building. He felt a large smile break out across his face as he realized that he loved that sound: the noise of a *beis midrash* filled to its capacity with those excited to plumb the Torah's depths.

He waited for the emptiness he had felt months before, the creeping doubt that had turned the singsong voices into black noise, but all he felt was light. And free. He hummed as he made his way past the coffee room — he'd grab a cup later — past the offices, and straight into the eye of the storm. Tears clouded his vision as boys called out to him "*Shalom aleichem!*" and "Welcome back, Rebbi!"

Rabbi Litkowitz looked up from his Gemara and smiled gently as his *chavrusa* walked toward him. "How does it feel, Reb Dovi?" he asked softly. He had agreed to join Dovi in the yeshivah's *beis midrash* for morning *seder*, something Dovi was thrilled about.

Dovi looked around again and blinked the tears out of his eyes. "It feels like I'm finally home," he said hoarsely.

And then they learned.

Two hours later, Dovi sat back and stretched. "Okay, I can use a coffee now," he said, smiling tiredly at his *chavrusa*.

Rabbi Litkowitz grinned. "You're not the only one," he said around a jaw-cracking yawn.

The two men closed their Gemaras and stood up. Dovi lingered an extra moment, stroking his Gemara gently. *I'm sorry I left you*, he said silently. He felt ashamed of himself for having abandoned his beautiful *chassan Shas*, but it seemed to forgive him. Just like the *kallah* who had given them to him...

He had barely downed his first sip when a *shana aleph* boy he didn't know appeared at his elbow.

"Rabbi Gordon asked if you can stop by his office," he said blandly, his blond *chup* bouncing with every word.

Dovi eyed the boy with interest, noting the brazen stance that belied the darkness in a pair of searching green eyes. *I'll get to you later*, he promised silently. But all he did now was clap the new kid on the back, thank him for the message, and get up to see Rabbi Gordon.

"Reb Dovi! Welcome back!"

The words were spoken with love and warmth, like a father welcoming a cherished son back from sleepaway camp. Dovi felt his insides melt and the last of his barriers fade away as he gazed at the older man.

"Rebbi," he said. That was all he could get out, but it was enough.

Rabbi Gordon came around his desk and embraced Dovi tightly. "Welcome back home," he repeated. "Welcome home..."

❧

THE ART THERAPY ROOM IN HEALTHWAYS was one of the program's finest amenities. Ten standing easels were scattered around the perimeter of the room, each one paired with a tall stool. The paint shelf had hundreds of colored bottles of paint lined up on it, and a cubby next to it contained brushes of every shape and size. The four walls were proudly covered with clients' artwork. There were the typical paintings: fruit baskets, sunsets, and flowers. But some of the paintings were more revealing, raw and harsh. Splashes of angry reds and browns pooled on a white background. A human heart, painted only in blues. Two hands, one minuscule, one larger than life. Broken shards of glass on a kitchen floor.

Gali loved the candidness of the room, the honesty and heart that poured off these walls, turning each canvas into a window into its maker's soul. She herself had never been artistic, but after watching her girls work so earnestly, almost feverishly, in this room, she'd found herself wishing, more than once, that she could paint.

She was passing the art therapy room now, having just finished a session with a client. She peeked inside. It was empty. Before she knew it, she had entered the room and perched herself on a stool next to an easel.

For a moment, she stared at the blank, white canvas in front of her, thinking of all the things she had wanted to be in life and all the things she could never have. She thought of babies and artists, families and dreams. She started when a tear splashed onto the easel. That wasn't part of the plan. Crying was for the old Gali, the Gali of many months ago. The new Gali, the one who had weathered difficult storms recently, was stronger and tougher, and she wasn't afraid of doing things she wasn't good at.

She thought for another moment, and then dipped her paintbrush into the green paint. Back and forth she painted, with a sort of frenzied drive, dipping and splashing and smearing, her eyes wide, her hands moving. And when the canvas was covered in color, it wasn't good, in the regular sense. But it was hers, and she was proud. She propped it up to dry and went to wash her hands.

When she came back, the sun was hitting her scene of a green meadow filled with elephants and one lonely deer standing nearby. But because anything could exist in her picture, there was a baby deer following close behind. And if you looked closer, the mother deer was smiling.

CHAPTER FORTY-TWO

The baby slept peacefully, her small chest gently rising and falling. Her tiny lips fluttered as each breath left her mouth, and she emitted a little sigh. Suddenly, she started to cry. Her wails reverberated around the room, crescendoing to a deafening pitch. She twisted from side to side in obvious distress. Her eyelids flew open to reveal a startling blue...

Gali gasped and sat up in bed, sweating. Her eyes darted around the room, looking for the crib, and her hands stretched out to comfort the tiny being. But it was a dream, just a dream. She dropped her head into her hands, her entire body trembling. "Just a dream," she murmured. It was just a dream.

She tried to fall back asleep, but the blue eyes of the baby in her dream haunted her. She could still hear her cries, and the intensity with which Gali longed to hold her warm, little body was so strong, it was almost painful.

She fluffed her pillows, adjusted the thermostat in the room via the remote, and finally just lay there in bed, eyes wide open. She thought over the past year, images flashing through her mind as if on a slideshow. Images of Dovi in jeans...of Aviva's angry face, her thin hands balled into fists...and memories of Yair.

Yair in the bath, Yair in his crib, Yair playing, Yair teething, Yair laughing. She could hear his laugh, crystal clear in her mind, the purity of its chimes so utterly haunting...

She knew she was crying even before the first tear fell, but the images continued. Ora Meyers at her Shabbos table, Avrami Meyers laughing coarsely, Dovi on his iPhone... Ora in her office, Dovi in a black hat, and Yair... Yair wrapped in a towel, fresh from the bath; Yair rolling from side to side on the living room rug; Yair spitting up...

Her face was wet as the montage slowed. Soon, it was just images of her. It was like having an out-of-body experience. Gali saw herself coaching clients...crying for her husband to return...sitting at conferences... She saw herself swaddling Yair...returning Yair to Shoshana, his true mother...and finally, she saw herself sitting in the doctor's office, darkness descending on her last hopes and dreams...

She lay there, exhausted, and had a sudden flash of clarity. She knew what she wanted. She pulled a tissue out of the box on her nightstand and dabbed at her face. She murmured *Hamalach Hagoel* one more time, and then she drifted off into a deep, dreamless sleep.

ﻉ

"Mmm, there is *nothing* like Israeli ice cream." Dovi sighed happily, licking a drop of chocolate off of the corner of his lip. Gali giggled, happy that he was enjoying her surprise. She had called him as soon as *seder* was over and had asked that he meet her in the park. She had picked up two of their favorite ice creams from the local *makolet* and brought them straight over.

She licked her cone and waited until Dovi turned to face her.

"Okay, Gals, now what's up?"

Gali looked at him, at her partner and best friend for so many years, and for a moment, she was afraid. This could be her only chance, her only hope; what if he nixed the idea? What if he laughed or said that it was impossible? She herself knew what a daunting process it was. Especially now, so soon after the trauma of giving back Yair, he might not want to start anything gut-wrenching again. Would she have the strength to move on after hearing him tell her that? Would she ever forgive him?

But she had to take the risk. And so she told him.

That night found them sitting at the dining room table. Gali had put out bowls of popcorn and nuts, and she was wearing a comfortable snood. Dovi had kicked off his shoes and had his sleeves rolled up. They were ready to work.

Gali had printed out seven applications. Each one was different. Dovi picked up the first one and turned to Gali. "You ready?" he asked, trying for a light tone. She nodded. He cleared his throat and read on. "'So! You Want to Adopt?'"

He stopped and turned to Gali. "You ready?" he asked again.

She smiled and blinked the tears out of her eyes. "I've never been more ready for anything in my whole life, Dovi," she said softly.

He put the application down and looked at her. "Then I'm right at your side," he said hoarsely. "I'm your teammate. We are in this together. One hundred percent. Okay, Gali? And it's going to work out! We're going to get a baby! Forget waiting lines and expenses. *B'ezras Hashem*, we are going to be parents. I just know it."

Gali said nothing, but the look in her eyes spoke volumes.

Dovi suddenly felt energized. "Ready?" he asked for a third time.

Gali laughed, a small shaky sound. "I'm ready," she said.

So he picked up the application again and continued reading.

CHAPTER FORTY-THREE

She had the distinct sense of déjà vu as they stood on the sidewalk and faced the store. She heard Dovi draw in a deep breath, and just by his very presence, she knew everything had changed since her last visit here. She stared at their reflections in the window. Ironically, she looked calm, while the bearded man next to her had a huge smile on his face.

Dovi adjusted his black hat. "This is it," he said. "All set to go blow a ton of money on a bunch of overpriced items, of which we'll probably only need half?"

She gazed up at him and then back at the store, a smile slowly breaking out over her face. They stood like that for another moment, smiling goofily into the store window.

Then Dovi said, "Okay, then, let's do this!" And they went in.

Three hours later, they arrived home, carrying in whatever was small enough to fit into the car they'd rented. The rest would be delivered to their home later on that day.

"We have newer models coming in later this week," the saleswoman had told them.

"We need everything *today*," they'd emphasized. Today. Because the baby would be arriving tomorrow.

The call had come the day before. Gali had been elbow-deep in suds, washing dishes, when the phone rang. Hastily peeling one dish glove off, she'd pressed speaker.

"Gali? It's Meytal."

The plate Gali had been holding slipped out of her fingers and splashed harmlessly into the sink. "Meytal," she'd breathed. The social worker of the adoption agency...

The voice sounded light. "I love this part of the job. Gali, we have your baby!"

Gali swallowed. "I'm listening," she choked out.

The voice was suddenly brisk. "Baby girl, born yesterday, 3.5 kilo — for you Americans, I guess that would be about seven or eight pounds. Yours was the next name on the list..."

"Mgrglh," Gali said.

Meytal laughed. "Gali, breathe! You've undergone two years of tests, evaluations, therapy sessions, and background checking by us. It all had to be for a reason, no?"

And suddenly, Gali found her voice. "Yes!" she said loudly. "Yes! So she's ours? Are you sure?"

Meytal laughed again. "I'm with her right now. She's yours."

Gali didn't know she'd been crying until the tears were falling off her chin and sliding down her neck. "Thank you, Meytal, thank you..."

The social worker's voice grew warm. "It's my pleasure, Gali. Really. I'll call later with more details. Oh, and Gali? She's beautiful."

෨෪

SHE REALLY WAS BEAUTIFUL. Gali looked at the picture Meytal had emailed her. A tiny pink bundle wearing a snug little hat. Gali tried to smile, to admire the baby's heart-shaped face and button nose. But she was afraid. She was scared to love her, to feel anything for her except a distant sense of interest. She wasn't going to open her heart until that baby was safely in her arms. And even then, she wouldn't believe she was hers until the six-month trial period was up.

But then, *if* she was still hers, then Gali was going to love that baby with a love so fierce, so strong, that no one would ever know she was not her own flesh and blood.

She turned to Dovi, who was on the floor sorting the baby clothing. "Dovi..."

She looked at him, but the words didn't come. Still, not everything needed to be spoken to be understood.

"I know," he said, looking up at her. "I know."

She threw him a grateful smile. Then she sat and folded soft pink undershirts until it was time to start thinking about dinner.

෨෪

THE APARTMENT WAS DARK, the only glow a shaft of moonlight that filtered in through the big living room window. The Jerusalem stars appeared closer than ever in the inky sky, and all was peaceful when a sudden cry pierced the night.

Gali sat up, disoriented. "What?" she asked, still half-asleep.

Dovi jumped out of bed, got tangled in the sheets, and almost fell over. "She...what...cry..." he mumbled, fighting with the blanket. Gali tried not to laugh as she slid her feet into slippers and went into the other room.

She bent over the bassinet. "Shh, shh, little baby," she said soothingly, scooping up the tiny, screaming bundle. The baby's cries began to subside, but Gali kept talking, her voice low and calm. "Mommy's here, little girl. Mommy's here..."

The baby grew silent. Her little eyes opened in a wrinkle of confusion and then closed, as if with relief. It was like she'd been checking to make sure it was her mother — and it was. Now Gali was the one crying, a mixture of relief, exhaustion, and pure joy.

"You look so natural," came a soft murmur at her side. She looked up to find Dovi standing there, tears streaking down his face as well.

"It *feels* so natural," she returned, sitting on the newly purchased rocking chair and staring down at the pristine perfectness of her daughter's little face.

"Can you believe that just a little while ago, she didn't exist, and we didn't know how long we would have to wait...." Dovi said, wonderingly.

Gali sighed, a deep sound of innate calm. She hadn't felt like this in over ten years. It was as if she could breathe at last, unclench her fists, and let go... Finally, *finally*, she could be who she was supposed to be.

"Well, here we are," Gali said, rocking her baby back and forth. "In the middle of the night, as awake and exhausted as any other parents in the world..."

Dovi laughed. "Hey, it's not very glamorous...but it's everything." Gali looked across at him, and they smiled at each other.

"Want me to take over?" he offered, knowing already what her answer would be.

"No, I'm okay," she said, looking down again at the tiny features. "Actually, I'm more than okay," she amended.

Dovi tried to say something else, but he couldn't, so he just nodded, eyes bright, and turned to leave the room.

"Say goodnight to Abba," Gali whispered into the baby's little seashell of an ear.

ಶ

IT WAS AS IF A GIANT PINK EXPLOSION had been set off in the dining room. Gali's mother, who had flown in together with her husband especially for their new granddaughter's kiddush, had gone slightly overboard, but no one could really blame her.

Gali adjusted the white crocheted bow on the baby's head and wrapped her in a light pink blanket. "Come, my sweet one," she whispered. "Let's go get you a name." The baby hiccupped in agreement, and they were off.

She stood there, amidst friends and family, as Dovi received an *aliyah* and the baby was named Reena. At long last, Gali felt complete.

The kiddush was beautiful. The grandparents *shepped* their long-awaited *nachas*, and friends and neighbors stepped in and out to wish the proud new parents mazel tov. It was long past noon by the time the last well-wisher had gone home, and Gali and Dovi were both exhausted and exhilarated.

Gali's mother ushered them to the couch, placed a cold drink in each of their hands, and told them to relax. "Reena'le and I will get acquainted," she said firmly, gathering up the guest of honor and leaving the room with her.

Gali and Dovi sat there together silently, allowing the moment to be captured for posterity in their hearts.

"*L'chaim*," Dovi said quietly, raising his glass and clinking it against hers.

Gali smiled, a wide, happy smile. "L'Reena," she said, and they both giggled.

"To Reena," Dovi agreed. "To our little ray of happiness."

"To us," Gali said, her tone now serious. Dovi looked at her. "For weathering the storms of the past decade...together."

He smiled too, a touch sadly, words teetering on the edge of his lips. "To our beautiful new family," he said at last.

"*B'chasdei Hashem*," she answered. And then there was nothing left to say.